A Sheriff

for Sophie

Lynne Lanning

1

Chapter 1

"Son," Mrs. Gentry pleaded as tears ran down her face. "All of this was a terrible accident. No one in their right mind would hold it against you."

William unbuckled his gunbelt and slung it across his bed. "I don't want to talk about it anymore, Ma. I am a shame and disgrace, and because of me, a beautiful young woman is in the doc's office hanging between life and death. If I don't give up my badge on my own, I will be more disgraced when they come to take it from me."

He gently pushed his ma out of his room and closed the door behind her. Sitting with his head in his hands on the side of his bed, he thought back on all the events of the day. How could his life go from almost perfect to total disaster in a matter of a few hours?

Myra had devastated him right before lunch when she broke off their engagement without warning. What was it she said? What was her reason? He didn't think he heard one word after she said, "William, I can't marry you."

She had left his head spinning and his heart in his throat. He had aimlessly followed her out of his office, numb, and not paying attention to anything.

Watching her ride away in her buggy, he remembered seeing someone stumble out of the saloon and fall in the street. That wasn't anything unusual around here anymore, but it was a little early in the day for it.

He walked that way, in a daze, instead of being prepared to be confronted in a fight. Rarely did he have to draw his gun, being known for handling things peaceably or with his iron fists. He already felt as if the wind had been knocked out of him because of Myra, and didn't have the presence of mind to reason with anyone right then, nor did he feel like fighting.

A big man stepped out of the saloon as William closed the distance of a hundred feet. The man staggered a step, putting his hand on his gun.

"Don't do that, mister!" William yelled and came to a halt, pulling his gun.

The man raised his hands for a moment and slurred, "It's alright, sheriff. I ain't gonna cause no trouble."

William walked toward the man, keeping his gun in his hand, but pointed downward when he saw the man complying.

The man stared at William for a moment, watching him begin to check the man on the ground and glancing around for any other signs of trouble. Seeing him occupied, the man laughed sarcastically and pulled his gun.

William raised his gun but was too slow. He felt a bullet whiz by him as the drunk squeezed off a shot. He returned fire, leaving the man in a motionless heap.

He heard screams across the street and ran to see a heart-wrenching sight. There lay a young woman, unconscious, in a pool of blood, holding a screaming, tiny baby.

The doctor was summoned and an elderly woman rushed forward to pick up the baby. William couldn't seem to break from his daze long enough to get someone to help move her to the doctor's office.

He remembered two men pushing him to the side, lifting the woman, and a man running from the livery down the street, screaming in panic, meeting the men carrying his wife to the doctor's office.

****

Judge Gentry sat at the supper table waiting for William to join the family. Growing impatient, he sent his younger son, Earl, to get him.

When they both settled at the table, William wouldn't even look at his father. He had the utmost respect for the man, as everyone did. Judge Gentry was known as being fierce but fair in all his dealings.

"Son, would you like to tell me what happened today? I've heard accounts from several people who agree that you didn't do anything wrong. The only negative thing I've heard was that you seemed to be in shock when you saw poor Mrs. Lindsay, not reacting as some may think you should have. Yet here we sit, with you apparently having some other account of the incident going through your mind. What happened that I haven't heard?"

William cleared his throat knowing his father would settle for nothing less than personal responsibility and integrity. "I was distracted, sir. I let my guard down for a moment, reacted too slow, and now it may cost Mrs. Lindsay her life."

"Hmm, and what was the distraction?"

His face reddened. "Myra called off the wedding just prior to this happening."

The judge sat silent for a moment before slamming his hand on the table. "That is unacceptable. You know you can't let your personal life affect duty. I see now why you are so upset, and guilt ridden, as you should be. When people of the town find out, they may see their account of the story differently."

****

One year later, William reflected back on that day as he read a letter from his mother. He could imagine the tears in her eyes as she wrote heartfelt words begging him to come home.

Mrs. Lindsay had recovered, and no one seemed to hold anything against him...except himself, and that opinion was getting lower every day.

The day he turned in his badge and rode out of town, he left everything behind, including his emotions. Still having a keen conscience for doing the right thing, he had picked up odd jobs with local sheriffs along the trail, helping to bring criminals to justice.

He chuckled to himself sarcastically as he folded the letter and stretched out on his bed in this rat hole of a hotel. "Just who am I trying to fool? I am a stinking bounty hunter. One of the lowest life forms to ever wear boots. Despicable!"

Laying back on the bed for a few minutes, he finally got up and took a good long look at himself in the mirror. His mother wouldn't even recognize the man he had become. His hair hung shaggily to his shoulders, beard down to his chest, and his eyes...they didn't even look the same. They once held a glimmer of light and joy, but now looked dark and empty, perhaps even cynical and dangerous.

"I've got to do something different," he mumbled. "This isn't me. I'm not sure what I should be doing, but I know this isn't it."

Looking out his window, he stared out over the town. People bustling about, women with children in tow, men loading wagons, everyone serving some purpose.

"That's what I need. I need to find my purpose." His eyes immediately rested on the beautiful little white church nestled under some ancient oak trees, sitting at the end of the street.

"Trying to tell me something, Lord?" he chuckled. "Yeah, I know it's been a long time, and You are right there waiting for me to return. I'll keep that in mind."

Not in any hurry to get back to his life, he decided to stay put for a few days and rest. Maybe he could think about what direction in life he needed to go. One sure thing, he was too disgusted with himself to continue on this path.

****

Sophie Collins yelled at her two boys to behave themselves and get washed up for supper. She was about at wit's end with no hope in sight.

Looking around in exasperation, she took the time to quickly thank the Lord for all he had blessed her with. She could be in much worse shape. At least when her husband died two years earlier, he had left her well off enough to take care of herself and her children.

Running the hotel and diner was something she loved, but it consumed all her time and energy. Her boys needed her attention, and she couldn't spread herself any thinner. It seemed every time she turned around lately, one of her neighbors was complaining about some mischief her boys had been involved in.

Since school was out for the summer, she had to worry about them every waking moment. She knew they missed their father, and she certainly missed the influence he had on them. He had been a kind, yet firm man, believing integrity was the most important thing in life. There was no way he would have put up with how the boys were acting.

She poked her head out of the kitchen to make sure everything was as it should be in the dining room. All the customers seemed satisfied, with the girls she had working for her doing a good job.

Hearing a clatter and crash behind her, she knew the boys had caused more trouble. Turning quickly, she saw that they had knocked a fresh pan of biscuits and a full pitcher of tea on the floor, while horseplaying.

Gasping, with tears filling her eyes, she put her hand over her mouth before she screamed and alarmed all her customers. She regained her senses as she marched over to the boys, taking each one by the ear and hauling them out the back door.

The preacher and his wife were walking by the alley when they saw her drag her boys outside and start wagging her finger in their faces.

"She sure is having a rough time," the preacher mumbled as he continued his wife in the direction of the diner's front entrance.

"Yes," she agreed. "Something needs to be done. Someone needs to help her. Other than remarrying, I'm not sure how anyone could help."

"Now, dear. Don't you think that is meddling a bit? Mrs. Collins should be able to decide those things on her own."

"Hmm, yes, I suppose. But with her working from before daylight until past suppertime every day, I'm sure she doesn't have the time nor energy to be concerned with finding a husband.

"Seems it would be easy enough to do. With all the unmarried men around here, she should be able to find someone decent. If someone doesn't help her soon, she will have two delinquents on her hands."

The preacher nodded as he helped his wife with her chair. "I may have a few ideas to help her with the boys. Perhaps a few of us can get together and keep those boys busy enough that they're too tired to cause trouble. Then she won't have so much to worry her."

Sophie immediately put on another pot of tea and mixed up more biscuits before attending to the mess. She brushed her hair from her eyes with her forearm and called out to the Lord silently, "Lord, help me!"

Looking over at Gabe, her oldest at nine years old, and Calvin, still her baby at age six, her heart melted. They needed so much more than she could give, but she had no idea how to change things.

****

Thankful that he hadn't taken up too many bad habits, William, now known as Will, finished his supper quietly and stood to leave the diner.

"Hey, Will!"

"Will turned to see a few of his bounty hunter 'friends' sitting at a table near the back, beckoning him to join them. They were a rough bunch, and he was disgusted thinking how well he fit in with them.

"Why don't you join us in a little while over at the saloon? We'll get a friendly game going and see how well we hold our liquor."

All the men laughed as Will didn't even crack a smile.

"Sorry. I'll pass. Enjoy your evening."

As he turned to leave them, one man in the group asked, "Did you see the papers in the sheriff's office? Denny and his men were posted sure as anything, and I heard they aren't too far from here. Plenty of work and reward to go around with that gang. Want to join us? We'll be pulling out tomorrow."

Will thought for a moment, then looked down as he answered. "Thanks for the invite, but I think I'll pass this time."

The men were shocked, never knowing Will to pass on any bounty before.

"You ain't sick are you? Never known for you to sit back and do nothing, or do you have someone else you're going after?"

"Nope, I'm not sick, and right now I don't have a plan. Just figure to sit back for a few days is all."

"Got your eye on a woman?" another man laughed.

Will chuckled sarcastically. "With this kind of life? No, I don't think so."

After a moment, he waved and walked away, realizing three things that had really hit him hard that day; three things definitely missing in his life. He mumbled to himself as he made his way down the street for a nice, hot bath, "I'm cut off from my family because of my pride. I'm cut off from God by my own choices. Maybe I do need to find a good woman. But is there such a thing? Aren't they all spoiled and demanding?

"I stand a better chance with my family and God. Maybe I should start there."

He entered the bathhouse, deciding to trim his hair and beard just enough to keep from looking quite so scraggly. Looking in the mirror, he knew his ma still wouldn't approve, but this was a start.

The next morning, he put forth the effort to go to church. He was miserable and had to do something about his life. Perhaps God was still willing to help him.

Chapter 2

Sunday was the closest Sophie came to having a day off. The cook would always make preparations on Saturday evening for the Sunday meal. The only thing Sophie had to do before church was get the fire going in the stove. Three girls and the cook's sister would hurry right after church and take over running everything in time for the diner to open at one.

Sophie hurried the boys down the street toward the church. She didn't consider them bad, just mischievous, but they sure had frazzled her this morning. Between Calvin needing his clothes changed again right before they walked out the door, and Gabe chasing a frog that ended up landing a big muddy spot on her skirt, she was a bit upset about being late.

Scooting onto the bench near the back, she sat between the boys and dared them to move. They knew she was serious when they saw a stick in her hand to swat them if necessary.

Calvin was soon falling asleep against her arm, and Gabe sat quietly twiddling his thumbs, making plans for after church activities.

As they made their way out of the church, the preacher asked her to wait for a moment. "My wife and I would like to speak to you as soon as everyone else leaves."

Panic lined her face. "Oh! Preacher, have my boys...?"

13

He chuckled and interrupted quickly. "Everything is fine. We just wanted to have a friendly chat."

She let out a sigh and smiled slightly as she nodded. "That would be fine." Holding tightly to each of her boys, she walked over and stood under a tree to wait.

The preacher's wife, Emily Faulkner, walked over to them. "Mrs. Collins, would you and your boys like to join us for lunch?"

"Well, ma'am, that is very kind of you, but certainly not necessary."

Mrs. Faulkner waved her hand and smiled. "Tsk, I know it's not necessary, but it would be a pleasure. My husband and I haven't had the chance to get to know you very well, with only being here for less than a year, and we would enjoy that opportunity."

The preacher joined them and reinforced his wife's enthusiasm. "Yes, please join us." He patted Calvin on the head and ruffed Gabe's hair. "We don't have any little boys around anymore and miss it."

Sophie relaxed and accepted the invitation, excited to have something other than work and her boys to think about for a little while.

She was really excited when the preacher and his wife asked for the boys to stay with them for the afternoon, giving her a chance to do whatever she wished. What she wished for was to sit and read more about this agency she had heard about and then pray about what to do. But could she be so daring to even consider it seriously?

She opened the package of information from a matchmaking service, finding a list of credentials and several testimonials, along with an extensive application. She had always been inquisitive, wanting to know every aspect of how things worked, so she decided to ask for that information packet and see for herself. Now here it was. What was she going to do with it?

She prayed as she began filling out the form, listening for the boys to return any moment. There was no way she could ever admit to anyone what she was thinking or doing. It seemed shameful, disgraceful, yet exciting.

Keeping her mind on why she was doing something so desperate and daring, she put all of the information away except the application. She held it in her hands as she prayed fervently.

Pouring her heart out to God, even with Him knowing her circumstances, she listed reasons for her plea. The boys needed a father; they needed guidance and instruction that she didn't have the time or knowledge to give. She continued on with every reason she voiced having something to do with her boys.

Suddenly, as if a voice had spoken audibly, "What is it YOU need?" came to her mind.

"I need help, Lord. That's all I know to say. I need help from You and a good man willing to come here to Nebraska and be a good father for my boys."

****

Will sat on the back row in the church, trying to stay unnoticed by everyone. It felt good to be back where he knew he belonged, well, at least in the house of God.

"One step at a time," he thought. "Lord, I need to get You back in control of my life and let You guide me. I hope you see fit to get me out of Arizona and see me safely back to Missouri."

Not wanting to be social, as soon as the last Amen was uttered, he made his way to the diner. He missed his family and wanted to visit, but there was no way he would stay there.

Even knowing the town would accept him back and held no ill will toward him, for some reason, home just wasn't inviting anymore.

He picked up a newspaper and read as he waited for his meal, with something so intriguing catching his eye, that he read it over a few more times as he ate.

28-year-old widow with some means, business owner. Seeking hard-working Christian man, 30-40, with integrity. Marriage required, romance not.

Just for amusement, he often turned to this section of the paper, usually only seeing where men had placed ads for a mail order bride. Here was a woman in such dire need, she was placing an ad.

He saw the ad was placed with one of the most well-known agencies, which he had heard were very particular about who they dealt with, requiring proof of everything you said before accepting your application. He had also heard they were expensive but delivered on their promises.

This woman must be serious yet particular. She could have placed a much cheaper ad if she was just desperate. He read over it again. Although he had just turned to this page for a bit of entertainment, he found himself taking this one seriously.

He shook his head and quickly closed the paper, but he couldn't get it off his mind. He looked at the ad again. It was as if the woman was describing him, except for the word integrity. He used to have that, but it seemed a thing of the past.

"I need to get my mind on visiting my folks and leave all this other alone before I wind up in trouble," he chided himself, before another thought hit him from out of nowhere. "Didn't you say you wanted God back in your life? This woman wants a Christian. Didn't you say you needed a woman and missed family life? Weren't you wanting a purpose? This woman needs a hard worker and a husband but apparently has been hurt before, not ready for a relationship. This may be your chance to find peace."

He closed the paper again and made his way to his room. "Sounds like a sure way to find trouble."

The next morning, he packed his bags and left for his parent's home. It was a long trip, with many miles and towns between. He figured he would stop in and visit with some of his sheriff friends along the way.

"Sure would suit me not to travel this way again. Better see anyone of interest while I'm passing through."

A few weeks later, he was wishing he had just stayed on the trail and not visited so much. His ten-day trip had turned into three weeks, with several of his sheriff friends needing his help as he passed through.

Every Saturday, he would be sure to settle for the night in a town, go to church on Sunday morning, and eat at the diner before getting on his way again.

He always picked up a newspaper on Sunday, reading as he enjoyed his meal, and every Sunday for four weeks, he was met with that same ad. He had tried to put it out of his mind, but then it was put right in front of his eyes again.

****

Just as he thought, his ma was upset about his long hair and beard, pulling out her scissors and threatening him. But it was worth hearing her go on a bit, just to be around her again.

Then she started about wanting grandchildren and that he needed to settle down.

He hugged her tightly. "It's nice to be home, ma."

His father was riding the circuit, doing his job as judge, and wouldn't be home for a couple of weeks. William wanted to see him and decided to take an extended vacation, helping out around the house while he was there.

His ma had him spoiled in no time. It was nice to have her doting on him, cooking and doing his laundry, everything that a wife...He caught himself. "Why in the world would I even think that?"

He supposed that between his ma and all the newspaper clippings he had collected from that same ad over the last few weeks, it was never far from his mind anymore. Shaking from his thoughts, he went back to chopping wood and doing chores for his ma.

"William?" she asked with a sparkle in her eye after supper one evening. "Would you please explain what I found in your pocket when I did your laundry today?"

She put a pile of folded papers on the table.

His face reddened. It was where he had seen and kept every week's edition of that ad, making sure it was still there. He reached for the pile and she slapped his hand.

"Explain, please? I see from the dates you have had this same ad on your mind for a month now?"

He didn't know what to say.

"Tell me, what has intrigued you so?"

He shrugged as his brother chuckled. "Well, ma, I just got to thinking about the whole thing, and I've prayed about it a lot, too."

He explained what he knew about the agency and their reputation, and what he had imagined about the woman by reading between the lines.

"Looks as though she is careful enough and has enough money to be a bit particular. Sounds like she needs help, perhaps with whatever business she owns, but isn't desperate enough to just accept the first offer that comes along.

"And it seems as though she's a bit lonely for companionship but is scared of getting her heart entangled. Ready to commit to a lifetime relationship, thinking with her head and not her heart. Sounds pretty smart to me."

His ma crossed her arms across her chest. "So, a business agreement? Not a real marriage?"

He shrugged.

"You cut off that hair and beard and she won't be able to help falling in love with you."

Earl about fell out of his chair laughing.

****

The agency was located in Boonville, just a little over a day's ride from Will's family home. He happened to mention to the deputy that was acting as temporary sheriff that he was thinking about making a trip there. Once again, he was met with being asked a favor.

"Would you be interested in riding shotgun from here to Boonville? Just a couple of times is all I ask. We have some valuable cargo being transferred from here to the bank in Boonville. Lots of farmland and cattle have been exchanging hands recently. The bank manager wants to send large amounts of gold and cash to the bigger bank there but divide it into two or more trips."

Will rubbed his chin and thought.

"It pays good, but I just don't have the men to spare right now."

Will sighed. "Yeah, I can do that. When can the first load be ready?"

"Thanks, Will. I will go make arrangements for tomorrow's stage."

Will walked away thinking, *"Maybe it wouldn't be too bad to settle down. I'm about tired of moving around so much."* He chuckled to himself and went to purchase what he would need for his trip.

****

Sophie started receiving letters from the agency, discreetly, in unmarked envelopes not using the agency's name. They passed along all the responses they had received on her behalf, leaving it to her to respond or not. The men responding had to fill out an extensive questionnaire with proof of identity, employment, and a few other things, knowing that it was very likely she would be asking for character references before she made any decisions.

Out of twenty-three responses, she declined them all. She was exasperated and exhausted. Keeping everything to herself, she only had time to go through the paperwork after the boys were settled in at night, and all her chores done for the day.

Mrs. Faulkner had come over several mornings each week and taken the boys to help her and her husband with some plans for the upcoming July 4th celebration.

The boys always came in for supper excited yet tired. They would tell her how they helped make things for some of the games. Sometimes they painted boards for the games or gathered pebbles to stuff cloth bags for tossing. One night they even told about a dunking booth they were helping to build.

Regardless of what they were doing, she was thankful that they were staying out of trouble.

That allowed her mind to wander to her dilemma about this matchmaking. Should she run the ad for another month? Weren't there any decent men out there in need of a wife, willing to relocate and move right in? All of the men so far had left her with a feeling of disgust, distaste, or outright distrust.

Most sounded too boastful to suit her, making themselves sound like such a prize that she almost laughed. She had several men in town try to win her affection over the last two years, and she squashed them quickly. Most men around here saw her as an opportunity to get rich quickly without making an effort; none seemed to care for her boys.

"Lord, You have given me a sense of peace about doing this, but I just don't understand. I'm trusting you to guide me."

The next morning, the messenger from the telegraph office delivered an important telegram.

Your presence discreetly requested at office – Boonville, Missouri.

"What?" she said louder than intended.

"Is something wrong, Mrs. Collins?" one of her waitresses asked.

"No, nothing at all."

What could this be about? How could she possibly go? Would she have to close the diner? Would she have to take the boys? How long would she be gone?

Suddenly she wasn't considering NOT going. She felt a stirring within herself that urged her to go.

That urge only grew when she saw Mrs. Faulkner walk in the door at that very moment.

"Mrs. Faulkner, I'm so glad to see you." She shook the telegram slightly. "I have just been informed of an urgent matter I must attend to, out of town, in fact, out of state. I'm in a flurry not knowing what to do."

Mrs. Faulkner motioned for her to sit. "Does this have to do with your husband?"

Sophie gasped a bit, wondering how Mrs. Faulkner could possibly know about her advertising for a husband, then she quickly realized the woman was speaking of her deceased husband.

"Yes." She answered knowing it was misleading, but not really a lie. It was about her husband, she hoped, but her future husband.

"How can I help, dear?" Mrs. Faulkner reached out and took Sophie's hand.

"I think I can hire enough help to keep the hotel and diner running, but I need someone to keep my boys. If I pay you to do it, would there be any way you are willing and able?"

"Your boys are a delight, quite a bundle of energy, but they are just being boys." She got quiet for a moment. "Let me speak with my husband about it. Meanwhile, you make your arrangements."

"Thank you," she sighed with relief as she sprung from her chair and hugged the woman.

Hurrying to the kitchen, she started talking with the woman who helped her cook, finding that the cook's sister would be more than glad to help. From there, she spoke with the man that helped with the hotel guests and found an easy arrangement there also. Yes, it would cost her some money, but it seemed the Lord was helping her by making a clear path.

In less than an hour, she had made all the necessary arrangements, even finding out the train schedule, and how much it would cost. She prayed as everything fell into place, "Lord, I'm putting feet to my prayers by making arrangements, but if this isn't your will, please stop me."

Within five minutes, the preacher walked in and sat down. She took him a cup of coffee as he motioned for her to sit.

"My wife tells me you have business to attend. I won't pretend to understand, and I certainly won't ask, but I assume it is of utmost importance.

"I do enjoy your boys, but..."

Sophie's heart fell, yet she tried not to show disappointment.

"I will need your permission to treat them as my own, and that includes letting them attend and help with the July 4th celebration, if you aren't here at the time."

She wanted to shout with joy and hug the man but quickly checked herself and replied, "You have my permission and my deepest appreciation."

She hurried to the train station and then sent a telegram to the agency.

Arriving Thursday – Hotel Recommendation

An hour later she received a reply.

Claremont Across Street

"Thank you, Lord."

Two days later, she was packed and boarding the train after giving the boys more instructions, warnings, and loads of hugs and kisses.

Chapter 3

Will's first trip with the stage was uneventful, but his visit to the agency was interesting. He returned from his trip to Boonville just a few hours before his father arrived home. He had just enough time to tell his ma of the ordeal he had been through.

"It was like I was speaking a foreign language in a top-secret society. I finally got to speak with the owner and explained how I truly believe the Lord has intended for me to marry this woman.

"Of course, I had to show all of my credentials and even my bankbook to him. Luckily, I had quite a bankroll in my account. The man's eyes went wide as saucers. But when I got the sheriff there to vouch for me, that seemed to set the man at ease. Sure am glad Tim's a good friend of mine from way back.

"Until Tim showed up, I think the man was ready to have me arrested or deemed insane." He chuckled. "But Ma, this is crazy! I haven't even seen the woman. She could have two heads or be bossy as all get out. What in the world am I doing?

"The man said they have never experienced anything like this before and had never given in to anyone so blatantly breaking the rules."

"What now, son?"

"Besides praying a lot and hoping I haven't truly taken leave of my senses? I wait." He slumped at the table and shook his head.

"They were going to contact her and see if she would come in person to handle this. If she agrees, they will let me know when to come back. If she says no, well, I've done what I could. They will let me know one way or the other."

Mrs. Gentry squeezed his hand. "Sounds like we need to have a prayer meeting.

"Oh! Here comes your father. Let's keep this between us for now. I don't want anything to mess up your time together, and he just wouldn't understand."

He nodded in agreement and went outside to greet his father.

Will was pleasantly surprised when his father almost insisted he move back home. Usually, Judge Gentry was one to say what he meant one time and then let it go, always levelheaded and practical. He wasn't forceful with Will but very welcoming.

It was enough to cause Will to wonder about what he was thinking of taking on. The woman he had set his mind on owned a business; where? What kind of business, and would he even be interested in being tied down to it? What were her expectations of him? Would he be so far from his family he would never feasibly see them again?

He almost broke into a sweat, excusing himself from chatting with his father to go out and finish some chores. He needed to think. But he had already pretty much committed himself to at least having this woman consider him, and it was too late to change things.

Earl came home in time for supper, handing a telegram to Will, laughing and guffawing, heckling him. "Your goose is cooked, brother!"

Will took the telegram and read:

Arriving Thursday

Sweat beaded on his forehead, under his eyes, and on his neck. Grabbing his bandana, he swiped at his face and neck as Earl continued to laugh.

Will took Earl's arm and pulled him close. "Not a word of this around Father. I need to figure out what I've gotten myself into before I cause him any more disappointment, you hear?"

"Sure," Earl answered seriously before breaking out into more laughter. "You're sweating as if you've just chopped down a forest! Seeing you squirm is all the pleasure I need.

"But seriously," Earl quit laughing and looked concerned, getting Will's full attention. Looking almost solemn, he spoke quietly, "I really hope, at least for your sake..." he paused.

"What, Earl? Just say it!"

"I just hope she doesn't have two heads!" Earl doubled over in laughter, slapped Will on the back, and took off toward the house. "I haven't had this much fun in a long time! Sure glad you came home."

"Funny, Earl," Will called after him.

****

Sophie checked into the hotel on Thursday afternoon, finding a message waiting for her from the owner of the agency. He would discreetly meet her in the hotel lobby at six and accompany her to supper.

She nervously got settled in her room and freshened up a bit. Her mind went from praying to doubting, with her trying to convince her heart and emotions to stay out of it. All she wanted and needed was a father and influence for her boys and some help from a handyman, right? She had stated clearly that she wasn't looking for romance. What in the world could have happened that the agency would call her here? Had they found a problem with her application? Had she been so picky that they were refusing to work with her any farther?

Entering the hotel lobby a few minutes early, she sat in one of the plush, overstuffed chairs, trying to look and act calm while fighting the urge to pace.

At six sharp, a wiry little man entered with a tall, stout woman on his arm. He spoke to the desk clerk before turning in her direction.

"Mrs. Collins?"

Sophie nodded and stood.

"I am Art Stiles, and this is my lovely wife, Enid." They extended their hands in a warm greeting.

"We would like to talk to you over supper, but because this is such an uncommon occurrence, it may take the rest of the evening to work things through. My wife has agreed to join us, partly for proprietary measures, but also as an advisor."

Sophie nodded. "Is something wrong? Or should I ask, what is wrong that would have you bring me here like this?"

"Please, let me reassure you that nothing is wrong, just unusual." He motioned her forward as Enid took her hand. "We have a lot to discuss, but I will start by reassuring you that all of your expenses for this trip will be reimbursed."

That was an intriguing way to start the conversation, Sophie thought as Enid led her into the dining room.

After they ordered supper, Mr. Stiles finally got down to the business at hand. "We have never had anything like this happen before," he paused. "A young man came to our office last week and presented us with a bit of an issue. We have checked him out thoroughly, finding him to be an upstanding character."

He glanced at his wife. "At first, we thought he had lost his mind." He smiled briefly.

"The man showed us where he had collected the ads you placed every week, saying he had prayed over them and knew you were the woman God was leading him to.

"Of course, we had our serious doubts, but he went on to show us all his credentials, and even his bank savings book. He is friends with our sheriff and had the man vouch for him."

Sophie took a sip of water. "I'm sorry, but I don't understand. Why didn't he respond in the normal and proper way? Is he a rule breaker or perhaps someone who feels entitled?"

"You see, that's where we had a problem also. I gave him the application and insisted he go through the proper channels."

He pulled an envelope out of his vest pocket, handing it to her as he went on. "He did conform to the rules, somewhat, by filling out the application and giving recommendations and credentials, but he insisted that we deal with him in person."

Enid interrupted. "My dear, he believes that the mail would be too slow, and fears that the weeks, even months of correspondence getting to know each other, may cause you to marry someone else."

Sophie looked at the envelope.

"That is his application and copy of his credentials and everything, except his bank information. But I assure you, he has some means."

"What kind of work does he do, and why would he leave whatever seems profitable to him, to marry someone and start over elsewhere? I'm sorry. He almost sounds like an outlaw with a big bankroll who is posing as a Christian."

Mr. Stiles smiled. "I assure you, he is certainly not an outlaw, in fact, he comes from a family filled with lawmen. He was a sheriff until last year, thinking there may be something else he would be more interested in. He has held several jobs since, drifting from place to place, and found that life to be unsuitable.

"He claims that after praying and going to church recently, he saw your ad and took it as an answer to his prayers. Being nervous about responding, he put it off.

"Continuing to see your ad over the next few weeks, he felt reassured this was the right thing for him. During a visit to his family, finding the office was fairly close by, he decided he couldn't put it off any longer, feeling a sense of urgency. He even agreed to pay your expenses for this trip."

Sophie looked at the envelope again. "I must say, if I wasn't so confused and overwhelmed, I may be flattered. He does understand this is more of a business arrangement. It sounds as if he's looking for romance. My heart is not involved in this decision."

Mr. Stiles looked sheepish. "Yes, well, we talked about that issue extensively. He agrees that romance would be a bonus but not necessary, at least at first."

Enid leaned forward. "He seems to think he can win you over with loving kindness, over time, but has agreed not to press the issue. He really doesn't seem to be a forceful man, except when it came to getting his application done in person. Otherwise, I would say he is a complete gentleman." She looked at her husband for his opinion.

"Yes, I agree totally. In fact, I must admit that once I fully got over thinking he may be deranged, I found that I really like the fellow."

Sophie relaxed and nodded. "Does he know I'm here, that I did agree to come?"

"Yes."

She looked around cautiously, "So, he could be here right now?"

"Let me assure you," Mr. Stiles smiled. "I don't see him anywhere, and he gave me a solemn promise to stay put until you agree to see him. I am to send him a telegram with your decision, and he will be here within two days, depending on what time of day he is notified."

They finished their supper with Sophie going over the application with them, asking questions along the way. When the dining room closed at eight, they moved to the hotel lobby, continuing their discussion until a little after nine.

Sophie stood. "I thank you both for your time. I will pray about this tonight and hopefully have my answer in the morning."

Mr. and Mrs. Stiles said their goodbyes and turned to leave, as Sophie went in the direction of the stairs. As the couple walked down the street quietly, they heard someone call to them.

"Mr. Stiles, please wait!"

They turned to see Sophie hurrying toward them. "I have made my decision. Please notify him that I will see him." She smiled and felt better than she had in a long time.

Still nervous, yet in a different way, she began to wonder if perhaps this could lead to more than business, and her boys.

****

Friday morning, Will told his family he was going to spend the day in town, visiting and such. His ma and Earl knew exactly what he was doing.

He checked the telegraph office as soon as they opened at seven, and every hour after until ten. That's when he got the news that he hoped would change his life and give him the purpose to which he sought.

The deputy motioned to him as he stepped out of the office. "Got time for another run today? The bank is closed tomorrow, and would be a good time to get this cargo moved."

"I don't know," Will declared. "I have just received notice of urgent business waiting for me in Boonville. What time is the stage due, because I am in quite a hurry."

"It's due before noon."

"Okay. I'll be ready. But if it's late, I have to go on without it."

Racing out of town, he found his ma alone, telling her the news quickly and excitedly. He threw his things together and headed out of the house...or so he thought.

His ma met him at the door, not letting him pass as she stood with one hand behind her back.

She pointed toward the dining room. "Sit."

"Ma, I don't have time for a conversation now. We've already talked about everything."

"Sit," she repeated as she brought her hand from behind her, holding a pair of scissors. "You want to make her fall in love with you or not? Looking like a wooly booger will make her turn and run, and if it doesn't, then she's looking for a wildman and won't be acceptable."

He thought for a moment. "Yeah, you may be right. Even if she has two heads, we don't want someone who likes a wildman."

Mrs. Gentry set to work quickly returning this man into her handsome son. "I will be praying for you, Will. Marriage isn't supposed to be taken lightly and is intended to last for your lifetime.

"I won't pretend to like this arrangement, and I've told you that, but I will pray for you. From what all you've told me, I have to believe God is trying to show you something."

Will hugged his ma and kissed her cheek. "Thanks, Ma. See you in a few days, I hope."

****

Sophie had sent a telegram to the Faulkners when she first arrived. This morning she sent another explaining her business would take a few days, asking for a reply about her boys' behavior and well-being.

The remainder of the day she spent collecting her thoughts as she shopped in this town that had much more to offer than back at home. She had brought nice dresses with her, but since it looked as though she may be facing a wedding, she opted for a new one.

Several times she had to get her thoughts back where they should be, on a business agreement, with her heart continuing to toy with the idea of letting emotions seep through. With this big of an undertaking, she had to keep her wits about her. This was a lifetime commitment, and this man was a stranger.

After supper, she retired to her room and took a nice long, hot soak. This hotel was luxurious, and she was getting a few ideas about updating her own. If she had a husband willing to help, she could possibly update some things. She was so relaxed in the tub, she fell asleep and didn't wake until the water was ice cold.

She spent the next hour going over the application again, reading her Bible, and praying before crawling into bed, feeling a sense of relief.

****

Will spent a sleepless night in his bedroll outside of the small roadhouse. He turned over again, hoping for a more comfortable position.

Thinking of his comfortable bed back home, he wished they had stayed in a hotel in town for the night. "Wouldn't have mattered anyway," he grumbled. Between his excitement and nervousness, there would have been no sleep regardless. Finally, sleep overtook him.

Getting everyone up and going ahead of schedule, Will climbed up beside the driver and kept his eyes and senses alert. They saw some men riding along the ridge for a while, and at one point, the horses seemed a bit skittish. Both things set Will's nerves on edge. He felt like a moving target but had made himself responsible for this cargo and even the passengers. He argued to himself that bounty hunting was better and safer than this.

Arriving in town shortly after noon, he climbed down and stood guard while the driver went for the sheriff and banker. His keen eyes didn't miss a movement, including some of the beautiful women stirring about in town.

Within thirty minutes, the cargo was moved, safely locked away and accounted for. He was almost a stone's throw from the agency, yet couldn't go there until the paperwork was signed and he was dismissed by the sheriff.

The sheriff politely asked Will to join him for lunch.

"Tim, I appreciate that, but I have pressing business to attend. Some other time?"

"Business at the agency again?" Tim grinned and slapped Will on the back. "Sure thing, some other time."

Will nodded his appreciation and hurried to the agency.

Mr. Stiles greeted him as he entered. "I barely recognized you without your beard and long hair. I'm sure I wouldn't have recognized you at all if it weren't for the way you always seem to rush through my door with such a commanding presence."

Will smiled weakly. "Sorry, but, umm, I got your message. When can I meet her?"

"Well, I will see what I can arrange. We weren't really expecting you until tomorrow."

Will didn't know whether to be relieved or impatient. He quickly chose to be relieved. "I'll get a room at the hotel and get cleaned up. Would you send a message to notify me, please?"

Mr. Stiles nodded. "Certainly."

Trying not to hurry through the man's door as he was accused of doing, Will politely left, then hurried to buy a new suit of clothes. Suddenly, looking at every woman from the age of twenty-five to thirty, he wondered if he was seeing the woman he intended to marry.

Chapter 4

Sophie noticed the stage pull up, looking in quite a hurry. She watched as the driver climbed down and helped the passengers, then scurried away toward the sheriff's office. But what she paid most attention to was the other man riding as a guard. He was handsome and had to be brave to take on such a responsibility.

She stood still and watched this man for a moment, totally mesmerized. He stood tall and straight, seeming to notice every move made. He didn't seem nervous at all as he held a rifle in his hands, with two pistols strapped to his hips. She summed him up as courageous, authoritative, and no-nonsense, just as her husband had been. Although that was to be admired, it had left her husband lacking a sense of humor and compassion.

She shrugged and moved down the street, looking in some of the shops along the way. She meandered through the general store looking for something special she could purchase for her boys. She picked up a couple of brightly painted spinning tops, then ran her fingers through a bucket of marbles.

Sophie noticed a little boy watching her and she smiled at him.

A man stepped up and chuckled softly. "I used to love running my hands through the marbles while I waited for my ma to finish shopping."

She glanced up at a man with broad shoulders, supposing him to be the little boy's father. It was the same man who had been guarding the stage. *"This must be his home,"* she thought quickly.

"Yes," she replied. "I suppose we have all been guilty of that." She nodded her head politely and walked away, still browsing the shelves.

Finally making her selections, she went to the counter and waited as the man she had spoken to finished his purchase. She noticed he had purchased several items of clothing, a small bag of marbles, and a few candy sticks.

He handed the bag and candy sticks to the little boy, then walked out of the store, leaving the boy alone with a woman, Sophie supposed was the boy's mother.

As she made her purchases, she overheard the woman and little boy talking about how nice that man was, and neither of them knew him. "Son, that is a true gentleman."

Sophie smiled and thought, *"Yes, that's what the world needs so much more of. I could only hope my mystery man is half as nice."* She sighed silently, *"I guess I will find out tomorrow."*

Returning to the hotel, the attendant handed her an envelope. Thanking him, she went to her room and opened it after setting her purchases on the table.

She gasped with excitement when she read that her mystery man was in town. Mr. Stiles was set to make introductions in the lobby of the hotel at six if she was agreeable.

Quickly writing a note of acceptance, she hurried down the stairs to find someone to deliver the note. She couldn't be seen going into the agency. It would be terribly embarrassing.

Tripping over her skirt, not able to catch her balance on the last few steps, she fell…right into one strong arm of the stranger from the store.

"Steady there, ma'am. Are you okay?"

He bent and set his armful of clothes down on the step and helped her stand completely upright. He noticed when she winced in pain.

"Yes, oh, I, oh!" She grimaced as she grabbed his arm with one hand and the railing with the other. "I'm sure I will be fine in a moment. Please, just let me sit."

He helped lower her to the step. "Let me at least get you to the chair."

She nodded and extended her hand for him to help her up, when suddenly, he picked her up and carried her to a chair in the lobby.

Shocked and more embarrassed by the moment she snapped, "That was a bit unnecessary, don't you think?"

"Umm, maybe, but I have learned a few things in my life, and one is how to treat a sprain or a break. Now, if you don't mind, I will take a look at your ankle."

Skeptical, she pulled her skirt smoothly, covering both of her ankles, feet, and all. "I'm sure I will be fine. Thank you for your help." Tears from a mix of embarrassment, disappointment, and a bit of pain, flooded her eyes.

He noticed the note still clutched in her hand. "Do you need that delivered, ma'am? I could at least do that. It seemed to be awfully important, causing you to be in a hurry. I'll be glad to get it delivered for you."

She started to hand him the note, then quickly drew back her hand. Thinking quickly, she regained her composure, with an excuse to have something delivered to the agency, without being embarrassed.

"Are you sure you won't mind? It just needs to be delivered across the street. My friend, Enid, works at the agency, and I need to get this to her quickly. It's an invitation for her to join me for supper."

He smiled and took the note. "I'll be glad to do it. You sit still until I return. I'll just be a minute, then I will help you to your room."

As soon as he went out the door, she got to her feet and hobbled to the stairs, calling to the attendant to bring some soaking salts to her room.

She made it to her room, slowly, and poured a pan of water, setting it on the floor while she began to unlace her boot.

Will entered the agency asking if there was someone named Enid that worked there.

"That's my wife, Mr. Gentry. How can I help you?"

"A woman at the hotel wanted this delivered to her. She seems to have twisted her ankle and I told her I would deliver it for her."

"Thank you."

"Umm, Mr. Stiles, have you heard anything yet?"

The man smiled as he looked at the note, knowing Mrs. Collins was the only one at the hotel that would be sending anything to them. "If you could give me one moment?"

He disappeared into a back room, returning within a moment.

"Thank you for waiting. Yes, it seems that everything is set for tonight. We will meet in the hotel lobby for introductions at six."

Will smiled. "I just met my wife, didn't I?"

"I can't say for sure, Mr. Gentry."

"Can you at least tell me her name? I mean, I am going to officially meet her in a couple of hours."

Mr. Stiles squirmed. "This entire thing has been highly unusual and has caused me stress. Can you at least be patient for a couple more hours?"

He nodded as his smile spread across his face. "See you tonight."

Returning to the hotel, he wasn't surprised that the independent woman wasn't sitting there waiting.

He saw the attendant with a box of soaking salt in his hand.

"I can take that to her. I need to check her foot anyway. Which room? And what is her name?"

The attendant stammered, "Umm, sir, I really shouldn't be giving that information, unless you're a doctor."

"I'm not a doctor, but I am a sheriff that has dealt with all kinds of emergencies."

"Well, in that case, Mrs. Collins is in room six."

"Thank you." He hurried up the steps, finding she had left the door ajar. He tapped on it and then opened it slowly.

She gasped when she saw it was that handsome man again. "My, you are persistent." She reached for the box of salt.

"Yes, ma'am. Your friend said that you should be in the lobby by six, but I really wanted to see if your foot needed to be attended by a doctor."

"How will I ever be ready in time?" she exclaimed as if he weren't even in the room.

He was sure that this was his future wife, and he had just carried his own invitation to the agency.

"Now let me see to that foot." He knelt in front of her and poured some salt in the pan, stirring it around with his hand.

Thinking quickly, he struck up a casual conversation. "Seems as though this place is right popular. I have a meeting at six in the lobby also."

"Y...you are meeting someone in the lobby at six?" she asked weakly as he eased her foot into the water.

"Yes." He smiled at her. "My name is Will Gentry." He extended his hand.

She slowly took his hand while shock took over her face and voice. "My name is Sophie Collins."

"Nice to meet you, I just wish it were under better circumstances. Now, if you don't mind, I will leave you to soak your foot. It doesn't look too bad. Definitely not broken.

"I need to get cleaned up and dressed for a very important meeting tonight. I've been traveling since yesterday morning and need a bath."

She smiled slightly. "Yes, well, don't let me keep you. Thank you for your help. I should be fine now. You go get ready for your important meeting, Mr. Gentry."

He nodded as he stood. "Since we are both supposed to be in the same place at the same time, would you mind if I help you down the stairs?"

"That would be nice, as long as your wife doesn't mind."

"What?" he mused.

"When I saw you at the store earlier, you were with a little boy, and left him at the store with his mother." She knew that woman said he was a stranger to her, but he didn't know that. She hoped for a reaction and wasn't disappointed.

"Oh, no ma'am. I don't know anyone here in this town except the sheriff. I just wanted to do something for that little boy. I don't have a wife yet. That's who I'm supposed to meet tonight."

She couldn't keep the corners of her mouth from twitching into a smile. "Well, I do hope it turns out well."

He smiled kindly, picked up his pile of clothes and left. She fell back on the bed and hugged herself, acting as giddy as a teen-ager.

"Oh, Lord, thank you. He does seem well worth waiting for. A gentleman, strong, kind, seems to like children, compassionate, and handsome. Maybe I could see some romance after all. Thank you, Lord, and please guide us through this evening."

****

Will was downright excited. Yes, she was a bit spirited, but she was in pain and was probably embarrassed too. He wanted to be coy enough that she didn't realize he knew who she was, but give enough information that she knew who he was.

She sure was pretty, had good manners, and was modest. He couldn't wait to learn more about what she expected from him, but the way he saw it, he didn't think he had anything to lose, except his heart.

He bathed and made sure the little bit of beard he talked his ma into leaving alone, was neat and trimmed. His new clothes fit perfectly, and he had shined his boots until he could almost see his reflection in them.

At ten minutes before six, he knocked on her door. When she answered, his knees almost buckled. She was wearing a beautiful, fancy, blue dress, that enhanced her hazel eyes. A simple strand of pearls hung around her neck, and she had her hair fixed in loose curls on top of her head.

He cleared his throat as he offered his arm, "Umm," he tugged at his collar. "You look too radiant to be meeting with another woman for supper."

"Why, thank you, kind sir. May I say you cleaned up really nice yourself?"

"How's your ankle?"

"A bit sore, but tolerable. Thank you for your concern."

They reached the lobby just as Mr. and Mrs. Stiles walked in.

"I see you two have already met." Mr. Stiles grinned.

"Not officially, Mr. Stiles." Will declared. "This beautiful woman fell earlier, and I was just helping her."

"Oh! Well, let me introduce you. Mrs. Sophie Collins, this is Mr. Will Gentry."

They turned and smiled at each other, barely realizing Mr. Stiles was still speaking.

"My wife and I would like to chaperone you during this first meeting to be sure that all goes well.

Since this is new to us, having people, actual strangers, meet for the first time without knowing anything about each other through correspondence, we feel it would be best."

"Yes, of course," Sophie agreed, never taking her hand from his arm until she was seated at their table.

They ordered their supper and eased into a conversation with Mr. Stiles initiating some of the things he felt important to get out in the open.

"We ask that you both be honest about your expectations of each other. There would be no reason to hold things back, which may cause trouble later. It's best to see if there is any point in taking this relationship any farther."

They both agreed, as Mr. Stiles brought out a copy of each application and set in front of them.

"Ladies first," Will motioned to her. "I need to know what you expect from me, where we will live, what kind of business you have, and anything else you feel necessary to tell me."

Sophie swallowed hard. "Well, the first, and most important thing, the thing that may put an end to this evening and any hopes for a future together, I have two boys, ages nine and six."

She watched for Will to shake his head, throw up his hands, get up and leave, or something, but he never even flinched.

"Did you hear me? I need a father and a role model for my sons."

"I heard you. You seem to think this comes as a surprise. Your application said you were a twenty-eight-year-old widow, so I knew there was a chance you had children. Please continue. I just want to know the whole story and take it all in, if you don't mind?"

She nodded and started again, telling him about her business, her needs and wants, and that she lived in Nebraska.

"You seem so prim and proper. Tell me about you growing up. I want to know what kind of foundation, so to speak, that your life is built on."

"Well, it is quite embarrassing to admit, but I hope everything said here will remain between us only?"

Everyone nodded.

She cleared her throat, drank a sip of water, then continued as her face reddened. "My husband was a lawman. He actually rescued me from my father when I was fourteen, not long after my mother died. My father is an outlaw." She ended in a whisper and dropped her head.

"I understand if that makes you ashamed."

He put his hand under her chin and lifted her face toward him. "Did you cause him to be an outlaw?"

She shook her head.

"Then you carry no shame for that. Please, continue."

"My husband was a wonderful, kind man, twenty-five years my senior. I loved him from the day he rescued me, and he finally married me when I was almost seventeen. He was shot soon after my oldest son was born and decided to give up being a sheriff. He bought the hotel and diner that I now own.

"I'd really rather not go back any farther in my childhood than that. My husband took over teaching me everything I needed to know about life."

"How did your husband die?"

"Excuse me?"

"I don't mean to sound rude, but I am a lawman, well, ex-lawman, and I like details. They tell underlying stories. I just wondered if it was an accident, sudden illness, long term sickness, and if you have truly had the chance to grieve properly. I want to know what my chances are of winning your heart, because you wrote that romance was not required. I think a true marriage deserves a chance for romance."

"Oh," she replied weakly, being a bit surprised. "As for how he died, he got sick two winters ago and died from pneumonia. I loved him, yes, but I'm afraid I'm not sure what you are asking about my grieving process and the chances of winning my heart. Do I miss him? Sure. Do I drag myself through each day wondering how I can live without him? No. I hurt for my boys though. They need a father. They need a man's influence."

Will nodded. He was beginning to think that maybe she had never really experienced romance. It sounded as though she loved a protector, a guardian, a father figure.

"What I expect of you is to be a father to my boys, a real father who loves them and enjoys being around them. Other than that, I need someone to help me run the business, do repairs, you know, things like that. I can't run my business from dawn until after supper and give my boys the attention they need."

Will looked concerned. "And without a real relationship between us, just a business partner and babysitter to your boys?"

"That sounds a bit harsh," she said defensively.

"I'm sorry, but we are supposed to be honest and voice our concerns, right?

"My concern is that I've been raised to care too much about people. I have a problem with being in a relationship where I know I will love you, because that's just who I am, without you ever feeling the same. I don't want you to regret the decision to marry me and be miserable. That would end up making everyone else, including me and your boys, miserable.

"I guess I just need to know if you will keep an open mind. I can promise to be good to you and your boys. I can even promise to love all of you. My decision is in your hands."

Chapter 5

Mr. Stiles called for a bit of a break and a few minutes of pleasant conversation while everyone had the chance to think about things already said. When they finished their meal and ordered dessert, he pointed to Will and asked him to tell more about himself.

"There's not a lot to tell. I guess I've already let it be known what I feel is the most important part of a relationship. Without love between a husband and wife, I feel like they are doomed to failure.

"But God is able to make love flourish, and there are times in the Bible and all throughout history where marriages were arranged but turned into loving, lasting relationships."

He sat back and sighed. "Okay, here's my story. I grew up in a loving home. Two God-fearing parents and one prankster younger brother. My father is a Circuit Judge, his father was a U.S. Marshal, and his grandfather was a lawyer. I guess you could say, it was in my blood to be a lawman of some sort.

"I was sheriff for six years in our town. I gave it up a year ago when a woman was badly injured because of my lack of paying attention. The folks in town don't see it the way I do. My father ingrained integrity and personal responsibility into me so deep, I couldn't get past blaming myself. The job is still available for me if I choose to take it, but..." he shook his head as he paused.

"Anyway, I took off, trying to find something else to do, somewhere where I didn't feel the shame of letting anyone down. I took some odd jobs, mostly with sheriff's offices across the territory, helping to bring men to justice."

Sophie's fork clattered on her plate. "You were a bounty hunter?"

Will sighed. "Yes, despicable, huh? And I got to where I despised myself after a year of running from God, my family, my town, and myself. It just wasn't me, and I was miserable. So I decided before I got any deeper in disgust and self-loathing, I needed to make amends with God and my family, which I did.

"I also needed to find my purpose for living. That's exactly when I found your ad in the paper. I had never taken any of that kind of thing seriously until I couldn't get my mind off your ad. It's like the Lord kept on me about it, then my ma found the ads I had clipped every week from the paper, and it fed her frenzy of wanting to be a grandma."

He chuckled. "She was already bad enough about it, but then when she saw it was on my mind, she ran with it. I guess you could say she pushed me over the edge with my decision to pursue you.

"And the rest, well, Mr. and Mrs. Stiles know all the rest. I was adamant about meeting you before someone else answered that ad. I already knew in my heart that even if you had two heads, you were the one God intended for me.

"But as I said, it's up to you. I can't force you to follow what I think is God's will. You are a Christian. Have you prayed about this? Is the Lord dealing with you? And I'm not expecting an answer to that, at least not now. I think we both have some praying to do, and thinking."

Sophie nodded. "Fair enough, but please explain about me having two heads."

He laughed and filled them in on some of his ma and brother's teasing.

The remainder of the evening went well, with no more deep conversation. Sophie told Mr. and Mrs. Stiles that she appreciated all they had done and that she thought they could handle things on their own from here.

Will offered his arm after the Stiles' left. "It's a beautiful evening and I would suggest a walk, but I don't want you on that ankle any more than necessary. Would you care to sit on the veranda with me?"

"Yes, I would like that." She wrapped her hand around his offered arm.

"Will, you're thirty years old and very handsome; why have you never married?"

"Well, I almost did. I had courted a girl for three years, and we had planned a wedding. In fact, her breaking it off with me that day, was the reason I was distracted and got that woman hurt."

"Oh, so just a year ago?"

"Yes."

"Well then, maybe I should ask you, since you have made it sound like you love so easily and deeply, are you over her, or are you still grieving?"

He looked at her shocked. "Umm, well, that's a very fair question, and I have asked myself the same thing several times this past year.

"I couldn't see it then, but I see it clearly now; she was in love with the position I had. She saw it as a position that demanded respect, and I guess she had tendencies to look down her nose at people. We had quite a few discussions about that.

"Seems as long as I gave her everything she wanted, catered to her whims, and she could demand respect from people, she was happy. But any time that I had to miss a function because of my job, she would get riled and stay mad until I bought her something new."

He shook his head in disgust. "I don't know what I was thinking. She really did me a big favor when she broke it off because I suppose I would have just stuck in there because I had nothing better.

"Anyway, I found out recently, the real reason she broke it off with me was because a new young lawyer had moved to town, and he made a lot more money than me. And that's fine, because like I said, I truly feel like she did me a favor.

"But that's why I'm cautious now. Even though I feel like God is leading me to you, I can't stand the thought of being in love alone, and I know it wouldn't take much for me to fall so deeply in love with you."

"Yes," she giggled to ease the tension. "Because I don't have two heads."

He turned to her and rubbed his knuckles gently against her face. "If it was God's will, I wouldn't even mind that. I would have two beautiful faces to kiss." He leaned in close and brushed his lips against hers.

She shivered as chills ran down her spine, pulling away from him slowly.

"We've covered quite a bit of ground tonight, Will. Perhaps it's time to say goodnight?"

"Sure," he said as he stood and offered his hand. "I can prove how strong I am by carrying you up the stairs if you like. Surely I will pass one of your tests about my abilities to be helpful."

"I don't have any doubts in that area."

"So, what are your concerns? How can I help ease your mind?"

She turned to him and stopped. "Will, I loved my husband, and we had two children together, but, I just don't know how to explain it. I'm just not sure what romance is. Sure, I've heard about it, and I suppose dreamed about it, but never really experienced it, and that unknown scares me.

"I am smart, practical, frugal, can handle a business, and make decisions, but I don't know what a romantic love is all about."

He gathered her in his arms, "I can show you. We can learn all about it together. I know how it's supposed to be from watching my parents, and there is nothing more wonderful than seeing their closeness to each other and knowing the security it gives their children.

"I want you to pray fervently tonight, Sophie. Pray about opening up and allowing yourself to love me."

He kissed her as he held her in his arms. She melted in his embrace and kissed him back as her arms encircled his neck, pulling him closer. She knew at that moment she had been missing out on something wonderful her entire life.

They both felt their hearts stirring, feeling this was the right thing to do.

He pulled back from her and looked in her face.

"We have some important decisions to make, quickly."

She nodded, hoping she didn't have to speak. He had left her totally breathless.

"Sophie, I know you need to get back to your boys. I would love to go with you and begin our life together."

She unwrapped her arms from his neck. "Yes, I miss them, and it's not right for me to stay a moment longer than necessary."

He nodded as he turned her loose and opened the door to her room for her. "I can't leave town with you or travel with you unless we are married; it wouldn't be decent. Yet, I don't want to see you leave alone."

He watched for any signs of what she may be thinking. All he could see was her flushed face and could tell she had liked that kiss every bit as much as he had.

Already bearing his soul to her, letting her know how he felt about expecting a loving relationship, he had one last step to take, and it may change his life forever. But he had already come too far not to finish.

"Sophie, I know it's crazy and really moving fast, but will you marry me?"

She gasped, and then her eyes seemed to sparkle. After a moment of silence, she smiled.

"Yes, I will. I promise I will be a good and dutiful wife, but Will, you have to be patient with me, teach me, and promise to love my boys."

"I can do that." He caressed her face and kissed her quickly before saying goodnight.

****

The next morning, Sophie woke with a smile on her face. She had sweet dreams all night and had no regrets or inhibitions. Suddenly, she couldn't wait to be married to this man who seemed to be so wonderful.

Dressing quickly yet carefully, she styled her hair and made her way to the dining room, looking around for Will, but not seeing him.

She went back to the lobby and asked the attendant if he knew of Mr. Gentry's whereabouts.

"No, ma'am, not really. Saw him leave about an hour or so ago."

She thanked the man and went back to the dining room to have breakfast, sitting where she faced the entrance so she could see if he came in.

Her ankle was feeling almost as good as new, and she realized she felt too happy to have any pain at all right now. She remembered that kiss, and a tingle ran through her.

Two rough looking men entered the dining room as she finished her breakfast and sipped her coffee. They didn't seem to notice her, but she thought they looked familiar. Then she saw a very familiar face and smiled radiantly as Will walked toward her.

He kissed her hand as he sat down. "Good morning, beautiful. How did you sleep?"

She continued to smile. "I slept better than I ever have. I hope you did?"

He nodded as the waitress brought him a cup of coffee. "I think you have become more beautiful than you were last night."

"That's sweet of you to say. Aren't you having breakfast?"

"I ate a couple of hours ago, and have been busy ever since. I hated not to be here when you came down for breakfast, but I'm trying to make some arrangements for us."

"Like what?"

"Well, I need to sell my horse if we are going to travel by train, but if we go by stage, I can take him with us, well, at least as far as my folk's house.

"Which brings me to a request. I've checked all the stage and train schedules, and if you could possibly put off getting back home by two days, it would mean a lot to me and my family if we could go by and see them before we head to Nebraska. I don't know when we will ever get the chance to see them again."

Seeing the look of anticipation on his face, there was no way she could refuse him. "I do need to get back as soon as possible, but seeing this means so much to you, yes, that is agreeable."

He squeezed her hand. "Thank you. The folks are going to love you." He pulled some papers out of his shirt pocket and began to show her the stage and train schedules.

"Think we can be packed and married by the time the stage leaves at ten? It's half past seven now."

She nodded. "If you can tell me your favorite color, I will see if I have a dress to your liking to wear for our wedding."

His eyes glazed over for a moment. "The one you had on last night was about the most beautiful I've ever seen. How about that one?"

"That sounds perfect."

"We need to get going. Let's get packed and check out of our rooms. I need to run down and get our tickets real quick, but it won't take me long to pack. I'll be by to get your belongings in no time, then we will go visit the preacher." He winked as he stood and helped her stand.

"I don't mean to alarm you, but please keep your door locked. Some rough men came into town not long ago, and a couple of them are in here right now."

Without glancing around, she replied, "Yes, I saw them. I will be careful, and I will let you know a secret." She paused before whispering, "There's more than a petticoat under my skirt."

His eyes widened just before he started laughing. "Smart girl." He walked her to the stairs and kissed her cheek before leaving.

Walking toward the stage office, he saw one of his old bounty hunter friends coming out of it. There was no way to avoid contact with him.

He looked at Will and couldn't believe how much he had changed. Although Will wasn't happy about the news he shared, he was glad for the warning.

Will walked into the stage office and only bought one ticket. His plans had just changed, and he didn't know how to explain it to Sophie other than just being honest, but not before he put a ring on her finger.

Chapter 6

The ceremony was simple and sweet, with every one of Will's words laced with sincerity. It touched Sophie to her soul, and she hoped more than anything that she could learn to love this man.

She prayed silently as she took her vows before God. "Lord, please let me be everything he needs me to be."

He kissed her gently at the end of the ceremony, leaving her wanting for much more.

They hurried down to the agency, telling the Stiles what they had done and promising to write a letter of recommendation for them. Will whisked her out the door and toward the stage, where he had some quick explaining to do.

"Sweetheart, I can't give you all the details, but," he paused and looked down at the ring on her finger as he held her hands. "I've got to send you on the stage without me."

She gasped. "Why Will? What's going on, and why didn't you tell me this earlier?"

"I promise to explain it all later. Please, just trust me. I will see you in a few hours."

Pulling her hands from him, she spoke through gritted teeth, keeping her voice low. "Is this how it's going to be, Will? Are you a different man than you made me believe? I trusted you."

He took her arm and led her away from everyone gathered, waiting for the stage.

"You listen to me. I haven't led you to believe anything that isn't absolute truth. I am asking for your trust, even though I understand your concern."

He saw she was seething.

"Dang it, woman, you shouldn't be worried with what I know!"

She crossed her arms over her chest and stared at him, not saying a word.

He blew out a breath in exasperation. "Okay, I'll tell you." Looking around, seeing that no one else could hear him, he began to explain.

"One of the men riding as a passenger is a U.S. Marshal. He is going to be guarding you and the other passengers. Seems as though a gang is likely going to try to rob the stage. I will be riding with a group of men, watching along the way for any signs of trouble.

"I wanted to be the one on the stage guarding you, but I'm needed elsewhere, and the Marshal is plenty capable.

"Keep your gun ready. How good can you shoot?"

She softened and answered, "Possibly better than you."

His worried look left as he smiled. "That sounds promising, and I will remember to find out someday soon. But for now, please don't be upset with me, and please be careful. This stage will never be out of my sight after it gets a few miles out of town. It has some cargo on it that is mighty precious to me."

He pulled her close and kissed her as the stage arrived and was quickly loaded. "I love you, Mrs. Gentry." He helped her in the stagecoach and sadly waved goodbye.

****

Sophie watched out the window of the stage nervously for any signs of trouble. Occasionally she would glance at the other passengers, three men and a woman, wondering which was the U.S. Marshal. Each of the three men were sitting at the other windows, all looking out as if on watch, so there was no way to know.

It wasn't a talkative group, and right now she was glad of it; she had too many other things on her mind. Why didn't Will say anything about this before they got married? Was he keeping other secrets? How well had the agency really checked him out? Exactly who had she married and what had she gotten herself into? Would she even want him around her boys?

The harder she thought about the situation, the madder she got. She almost wished someone did try to cause trouble for the stage, then at least she would know he was telling the truth.

They rode for several hours before stopping and taking a short rest. One of the drivers threw a sack of

67

sandwiches down to one of the male passengers to hand out to everyone.

"There's a barrel of water on the back," he pointed. "Help yourself." He climbed down and proceeded to fill a bucket for the horses to drink, while the other driver stayed up top, watching for any signs of trouble.

After fifteen or twenty minutes, they loaded back up and continued their trip, being bounced and jostled until Sophie felt her insides would never recover. She was sure she would taste dirt and grit for days with all the dust that was coming through the windows, yet, they couldn't see out if they pulled the curtains.

Just before suppertime, the stage pulled up to a quaint but decent roadhouse for the night. A man and woman greeted them and motioned them in for a delicious supper.

Sophie and the other woman were shown to the room they would be sharing for the night, with basins of water for them to freshen up.

"What a relief!" the woman passenger exclaimed. "I thought I would die before this day was finished. I think the drivers intentionally hit every bump they possibly could!"

Sophie laughed. "I agree." She poured water in the basin and sighed as she washed her face and neck. "I never knew a basin of water could be such a relief."

"My name is Carmen." The woman introduced herself and extended her hand.

"Nice to meet you. My name is Sophie. How far are you going?"

"Well, I'm not sure. I'm supposed to be going to Wyoming to meet my husband-to-be." She looked down in embarrassment. "But I'm getting weary of the travel and a bit nervous about the meeting."

Sophie sighed and patted Carmen's hand. "I hope everything works out well for you." She didn't dare tell her that she had just stepped in what looked like a mess of her own. Less than twelve hours ago, she had taken her own vows and now had no idea where or even who her husband was.

"Let's go eat and try to get a good night's sleep," she suggested, motioning toward the door.

Later that night, tossing and turning in bed, she wondered about everything that had happened, and how much she could believe. Will had told her they were going to see his family and that they would meet them when they got off the stage tomorrow afternoon. Was that the truth or was she going somewhere only to be stranded? And what purpose would that serve?

She thought about Will. He had been so kind and sweet. Was she a fool for having doubts about him or for believing him? All she wanted right now was to go home to her boys and forget this week had ever happened. But she couldn't get his face, his voice, or his kiss off her mind.

Tears came to her eyes. She turned toward the wall and prayed until sleep finally overtook her.

****

Mid-afternoon, the stage stopped with the driver announcing her arrival. She stepped off the stage after saying a quick goodbye to Carmen.

"I wish you the best of everything, Carmen." She squeezed her hand and exited.

Since she was the only woman getting off the stage, and there was only one couple with a young man standing as if waiting on someone, she supposed these were her new in-laws. Approaching them with a bit of apprehension, she pasted on a smile.

"Mr. and Mrs. Gentry?" she asked.

Before she got the words out of her mouth, Mrs. Gentry had moved forward and embraced her tightly.

"Oh my! Aren't you something?" Mrs. Gentry finally let her go and held her back to take a better look. "You are absolutely beautiful, my dear!"

Mrs. Gentry introduced her husband and Earl, then instructed Earl to get her bags and take them to the buggy.

"Where's William?" Mr. Gentry asked after greeting her warmly.

"He was detained, sir, but should meet us soon." Sophie couldn't hide her disappointment. "I was hoping he was already here."

"Detained? On his wedding day?" Mr. Gentry looked concerned. "I'm sorry, but I would like more information. It must have been something really important."

"Well, yes sir, it was, or so he said."

Mr. Gentry's eyebrows creased. "I suggest you tell me what you know."

Although the man seemed to be trying to keep a pleasant tone, Sophie almost felt intimidated. She looked around to make sure no one else heard their conversation before giving him as much detail as she could.

"Earl," Mr. Gentry called out. "Take your mother and Sophie to the house. I need to speak with the sheriff and find out what is going on." He marched away without another word.

Mrs. Gentry was concerned, yet trying not to let it show. She wrapped her arm around Sophie and led her to the buggy. "Don't you worry, dear. We will find out what's going on. Let's get you settled in. I know you must be tired and surely wanting to freshen up."

"Yes, ma'am. Thank you." She wanted to ask more about Will but didn't know how without seeming to doubt him.

Mrs. Gentry put Sophie at ease quickly, knowing just what to say, and filling her in on a lot of Will's background.

Earl was pleasant and mannerly, so much like Will had been. She could tell he had a sense of humor and was holding back from letting it show too much.

The next couple of hours almost flew by for her as she was welcomed and made comfortable. Conversation flowed easily between the two women as they worked together to make supper. Mrs. Gentry did love to talk about her family, and Sophie was learning a lot about this man who had begun to find a place in her heart, until Sophie noticed the woman seemed a bit nervous.

"Mrs. Gentry? Is something wrong?"

The woman turned and faced her. "Yes, there is. I just don't know what, and I'm tired of acting like everything is fine when I'm worried sick.

"This isn't like Will to do something like this. He was too excited about meeting you, and he must have liked you, I mean, you did get married. So something has to be wrong.

"With my husband taking so long to come home, it causes me even more concern. Worrying won't help, and I know our time is limited, so please, distract me by telling me about yourself."

Sophie put her hand on Mrs. Gentry's shoulder. "Ma'am, maybe we should pray about whatever is going on?"

Seeing Sophie's sincerity, Mrs. Gentry calmed a bit as she sighed. Her eyes softened, and she knew at that moment, Sophie was everything she had wished for her son, even though she knew nothing more about her.

"Yes, please, let's do that right now."

After praying for several minutes, they wiped their tears and finished preparing supper.

"Sophie, please tell me about yourself. I've rambled on about Will to the point of being rude. I want to know who you are and what caused you to accept my son."

Sophie swallowed hard. "Ma'am, please don't take offense. I do take my marriage vows seriously, but there was one main reason I accepted Will's proposal; he promised to be a good father to my two boys."

Mrs. Gentry gasped.

Sophie hurried on, "And I really need to get back to them. I had no idea I would be gone this long." She finished and stood nervously, waiting for Mrs. Gentry's verbal response. Prepared for a tongue lashing about roping her son into a ready-made family, Sophie felt herself turning red, wishing the woman would just say something.

After what seemed forever, Mrs. Gentry took Sophie's hands. "I have grandsons?" she asked sweetly as her eyes misted.

Letting out a big sigh of relief, Sophie smiled and nodded. "Yes, Gabe, nine, and Calvin, six. They are staying with our preacher and his wife during my absence. I must admit, I miss them more than I thought possible, and I've been gone longer than I intended."

"I understand, dear. I hope all of this matter will be cleared up and let you rejoin your boys soon. I would love to meet them."

Sophie took Mrs. Gentry's hands. "I would love for you to come visit. It's just a two-day train ride from here. You will be welcomed guests in my hotel."

"Hotel? You own a hotel?"

"Yes, ma'am, and a nice diner."

"Please tell me more. I have so much to learn about you."

It was way past dark when Mr. Gentry arrived home. He declined supper, saying he had eaten with some men while they planned their next move.

"What do you mean? What's going on?" Mrs. Gentry asked with alarm.

"Now dear," he patted her shoulder. "Don't worry yourself. You know I don't share official business with you, and you also know that I will take care of everything; I always do."

He started to walk away. "I have a few things to get ready for a trip that is necessary. I will be leaving at first light."

"Excuse me, sir." Sophie knew she wasn't supposed to question a man, especially her new father-in-law who was also a judge that expected the utmost respect. But her temper started to flare when the man had dismissed his wife so nonchalantly, knowing she had to be terribly upset about her son.

"My husband is missing, and I feel I have the right to know what is being done about it and any information you have found." She gulped hard as her heart pounded, but she was determined to stand her ground.

Mr. Gentry turned and looked at her firmly. Earl quickly excused himself to go find some chores to do. Mrs. Gentry came up beside Sophie and put her arm around her.

"It's okay, dear. My husband and his men will take care of everything. Sometimes it's best we don't know everything." Mrs. Gentry started guiding Sophie back into the kitchen.

"No, Mrs. Gentry. I have been hit with one bad surprise after another since I married Will thirty-six hours ago. I haven't even seen him since! I deserve and demand some answers. I have to know how to proceed with my life.

"I have two boys waiting for me to return home. Should I just forget all of this ever happened?" She pointed to Mr. Gentry, "Perhaps have you annul our marriage and be done with it?

"Or is he in danger, perhaps hurt, and I should offer assistance? I have to know how to proceed! If you won't tell me, I will go see the sheriff and demand answers from him."

Mr. Gentry looked at her for a moment. He had always protected his wife from anything unpleasant, and what he had just found out was as unpleasant as it got. He couldn't cause his wife this kind of worry until he had more facts or some answers, regardless of how demanding this young woman was. She had no right to demand anything. His son had married her, but it was in name only so far; they had no attachment to each other and were basically still strangers.

He spoke evenly, calmly, and full of authority, exactly like the judge he was. "Young lady, I think it would be best if you go home to your boys. Leave us your information so we can contact you. I will have Earl take you to the train in the morning and purchase your ticket.

"Be ready to leave about quarter past seven. The train headed west leaves around eight." He turned without another word and went to his room.

Sophie stood with her mouth gaped, watching him walk away, not believing how he had just dismissed her.

Chapter 7

Sophie arrived home, still spewing, worried, and definitely confused. She had prayed for the Lord to help her, and she found that help in the comfort of having her boys in her arms.

The last ten days had turned her world upside down and had profited her nothing. The best she could do right now was to pretend it had never happened...but she couldn't.

Will had gripped her heart like she never imagined possible, and something awful had happened to him. Something so awful that his father wouldn't even share with his mother, but surely that meant he was still alive.

She tried to concentrate on every word her boys were telling her about their adventures while she was gone. But her mind kept wandering to dark places she had thought long forgotten.

Thankfully, it was almost time for the boys to go to bed and she wouldn't have to pretend with her emotions any longer. She kept pushing away the memories of things she had seen her father do to people when she was just a child. The methods of torture he had used on people, men and women both.

A sick feeling overcame her. Yes, maybe Will was still alive, but there were things that were worse than death. "Lord, please don't let him suffer," she cried out in her prayers that night.

****

Judge Gentry and four other men met up with the local sheriff on the second day of travel. The sight before them was grim.

The sheriff greeted them as they dismounted. "Judge, everything is pretty much like we found it." He waved toward a wagon. "We just now got the wagon here to tote the bodies back to town."

"How many, and do you recognize them?" There was a slight quiver in the judge's voice.

"Six men and two horses." He walked along and pointed. "I'm sure I have paper on four of them. That man over there was in my office a few days back, don't know his name, but he was a bounty hunter after the Denny gang.

"Your son used to ride with them, and I saw him pull out with them the other morning. They had intentions of protecting that stage from a heist they had heard about, while of course, trying to earn the bounty.

"A U.S. Marshal was on the stage protecting the travelers. Will had tried to trade places with the Marshal, saying that his wife was on the stage. I do hope she made it to her destination safely?"

"Yes, she did. But you say Will used to ride with them? My son, Will, was a bounty hunter?"

"Yes, sir, and good at it. Haven't seen him around for a while though."

"Well, we have work to do. I need to find my son, and we need to find the rest of this gang. Will had just married the morning of this incident, so I'm sure he would have come to meet her if he was able."

****

"How did they know we were going after the stage?"

"Shut up, Shorty. Boss don't need no noise from you while he's nursing that head of his."

Old man Denny, known to all as Boss, opened his eyes a crack. He mumbled, "Send someone to get Junior and Sonny. Tell them what happened and tell them I'll be holing up for the winter with their sister. It's about time she took care of her pa for a while."

****

The 4th of July celebration was delightful. For a change, there was so much merriment, Sophie actually got caught up in it and had a good time. The boys drug her from one activity to the next, informing her of everything they had helped build, paint, or gather.

Gabe volunteered to be in the dunking booth for a while, enjoying every moment of being wet. He would heckle the person throwing the ball at the target, looking forward to being dunked again.

Mrs. Faulkner walked up and joined her as she watched Calvin bob for apples. "I'm so glad you made it back in time to join us. The boys were worried you would miss it. I do hope your business went well?"

Sophie smiled but shook her head. "No, I hate to say that it didn't. It was probably a wasted trip, and an expensive one also. I sure missed my boys too."

"Be assured, your boys were a delight. If there's any way we can help you, Mrs. Collins, we are here for you. We understand your dilemma of trying to run a business and raise your boys. We will be glad to watch the boys to give you a break occasionally, but dear, have you considered perhaps remarrying, having a man to share your burdens?"

Giving her a teasing grin, Sophie replied, "Yes, I have thought about it, and even entertained a few gentlemen briefly. I even had a rich man try to win me, until he let it be known that he intended to send my boys away to a prestigious boarding school. We didn't even make it through supper before I sent him on his way."

She looked around for a moment, making sure she still saw both her boys. "I am a package deal, and most men don't want to take the entire package.

"I did come really close to giving my heart away to a wonderful man, but apparently, he was too good to be true."

"What happened?"

"He disappeared. I don't know what happened to him. He was willing to take on my boys and give me time to sort things out in my heart. I don't know if he got hurt, died, or just changed his mind. All I know is he seemed perfect, and he's gone."

"Mrs. Collins, I'm so sorry. Please, remember, if there is anything we can do to help, you just let us know."

Sophie nodded her thanks and wiped the unbidden tears from her eyes.

****

The young Indian man took him to the top of the ridge and pointed down. "Big fight there. Six men die. You hurt. You live."

"You say I came from that direction?"

"Yes. Going fast, that way," he pointed. "Chasing men."

He shook his head. He couldn't remember a thing about any of it. He couldn't remember who he was or where he had come from, what kind of life he lived, or even if he was a good guy or a bad one in the fight that had taken place.

The only clues he had were a stub of a stagecoach ticket, two train tickets, enough money to last a while, and a shiny, new looking wedding band on his finger. He had two pistols strapped on him and a rifle on his horse.

The Indians had taken him in and nursed him back to health, and he had no idea how long he had been there before he was awake and able to keep track of days. That started three weeks ago.

Now he had to decide which of these paths to follow for answers after he figured out exactly where he was. The Indians had told him about a town close by, and he figured to start there by getting his bearings.

He nodded a thanks to the man and started toward town.

****

Judge Gentry found himself consoling his wife again. "Sweetheart, Will is going to be fine. The men we found that were with him said they saw him ride away. Yes, they thought he was hurt, but we scoured that entire countryside and found nothing. If he was hurt, it couldn't have been that bad to continue riding that far."

"But he would have come home or gone to Sophie by now. Something is terribly wrong."

"Sweetheart, listen to me. I know you took a liking to Sophie, but that young woman was a mite spirited. Will may have had second thoughts. He had stayed away from home for a year before all of this. I still say he's fine, somewhere, and probably doesn't realize we are worried."

Mrs. Gentry pulled away from him. "I don't agree with you on most of what you just said. Sophie may be a bit spirited, but not in a bad way. She was scared for Will's sake. I dare say I would have been a lot worse if I had been her.

"As for Will, maybe he is still alive. But you know as well as I, even when he was drifting, he always sent a letter before now. He knew you would find out about that incident. He wouldn't leave us to worry intentionally."

He knew she was right, but he couldn't bring himself to truly believe his son was out there hurt somewhere.

****

Sophie had sent and received telegrams and letters from Mrs. Gentry, both agreeing to let the other know immediately if Will showed up.

It was a relief to know that school would soon start again and keep the boys occupied for the biggest part of the day, and the days would get shorter, keeping them inside more, leaving less time for mischief.

The hotel was almost empty during the winter, and business in the diner slowed quite a bit also. She was ready for a bit of a break. Even though there wasn't a lot of income during the winter, she would gladly trade it for having her boys inside with her, knowing where they were and what they were doing, and even enjoy helping them with their studies.

Will had been gone, missing, hurt, or perhaps dead, for six weeks. Her heart still skipped a beat when she thought about him kissing her, but she knew with each passing day, there was less chance of him returning. She had resigned herself to staying alone and raising her boys the best she could. She had done everything she knew to do, and failed, now it was time to stop licking her wounds and move forward...her boys depended on her. That was her driving force, her reason for living.

****

Will rode into a lawless little town where nothing looked familiar. He stayed in the shadows and to himself. Was this where he had started from the day of the fight? For some reason, he didn't think so.

There was nothing here to hold anyone for long. He couldn't imagine any reason to stay, but tonight he would bed down on the outskirts somewhere and take a closer look in the morning.

As he mounted his horse to leave, a man stumbled out of the saloon as if being pushed and fell to the street. Suddenly, Will's head began to hurt, and a scene flashed through his mind. It was such a fleeting thought; he couldn't make sense of it.

"Guess I've seen that kind of thing plenty of times." He moved his horse in the opposite direction to look for a place to make camp for the night.

The next morning, he went to the small outpost, picked up a few supplies, and asked for directions to the town printed on the tickets he had in his pocket.

He was glad to find it was only a half day's ride, and made haste to put the miles behind him.

As he rode away, he noticed some men standing around doing nothing, except staring at him. They looked to be a troublesome lot. He ignored them and went on his way, planning to stay out of sight as much as possible in case they decided to keep him company...and they did.

Will sat beneath some trees, chewing on jerky as he watched the three men gallop past him. Just as he thought, they weren't too smart. But he was sure there was a fourth man with them in town, so he moved farther back into the trees and waited.

"There's the smart one of the bunch," he thought as he watched a man trying to find any trace of a trail. Will didn't take to being hunted, especially by such a gangly lot. He finished his jerky and decided to be the hunter, instead of the hunted.

Moving silently among the trees, he worked himself behind the man and threw a stick in the opposite direction. The man pulled his gun and dismounted. Within seconds, Will had the man on the ground, bound and gagged.

For some reason that he couldn't explain, he decided to take this man in and see if there was a bounty on him, instead of leaving him for his friends to find.

"Why not?" he shrugged to himself. "I've already done the work."

A few hours later, Will rode into town with his prisoner in tow. The sheriff wasn't in, but the deputy was glad to help.

"Yes, sir, we have paper on him." The deputy took the man and locked him up. "Let me just get your signature here, and I will give you the reward."

Will looked at the paper and hoped his name would come back to him. After a moment of just staring at it, he signed an 'X'.

Stepping out in the sunset, he saw that this was a nice size town, seemingly neat and orderly. He noticed the hotel and walked his horse over to it, keeping his eyes open for the other three friends he had made. Everything seemed vaguely familiar. Maybe he could find some answers here.

****

"Boss, time's moving on. Winter could move in anytime now, it being September."

"Yeah, as soon as the boys get back, I'll be ready to head on for a nice long visit with my daughter."

When the boys came back announcing that one of them had been captured and was sitting in jail, Boss had a fit.

"Who was it that got him? The sheriff?"

"Nah, one of those bounty hunters that we tangled with a couple months back."

Boss grunted. "Be ready to ride in the morning before we lose anyone else. We'll meet up with Junior and Sonny before long, then we'll show them all something, after we've had a nice long winter vacation, all expenses paid." He laughed cynically.

****

It had been ten weeks today since she married Will and lost him, all within a couple of hours. She didn't remember dragging around this bad when her first husband had died. She was having trouble getting over this, and she knew it was because of the feelings Will had stirred in her that no man had ever done before. How in the world could she have been what she considered happily married for nine years yet have deeper feelings for a man she didn't even know?

She started her morning routine of getting the diner opened for business and getting the boys up and ready for school. Stepping outside as she unlocked the front door, she breathed in the crisp air. Winter could be upon them at any time, but so far it had held off and she was thankful.

Looking forward to the winter months so her workload wasn't as heavy, she still didn't like the thought of so much snow. She knew once it started, it wouldn't let up for months.

The morning had gone well, with nothing out of the ordinary happening. She told her waitresses that she would return shortly as she made a run to check for mail, telegrams, and a few other errands.

When she returned an hour later, she barely noticed the crowded dining room while making her way to the kitchen to open her mail.

Suddenly she heard a man call out, "Sophie!"

She knew that voice, and it struck terror in her heart.

Chapter 8

Will stayed glued to his room except for taking his meals in the dining room of the hotel. Everything seemed so strange. It was like he could remember, yet couldn't. He was sure he was on the edge of getting over whatever had happened to him. He hadn't seen the men who had been looking for him and had kept watch out his window almost constantly.

One night as he sat in the shadows in the back corner of the dining room, he saw a wiry little man and a tall, stout woman come in for supper. He knew them, or at least he felt sure he did. How could you forget a couple like that?

He thought until he had a headache. Maybe he should just approach the man and say something. But wait, what if he was hiding from the law and this man would turn him in? For some reason, that just didn't seem likely. He had to know; he had to take that chance.

Standing, he put the money for his meal on the table and walked to the couple.

"Excuse me, sir?"

The man looked up and his smile went wide as he stood. "Mr. Gentry. How are you?" He extended his hand as he went on hurriedly. "I didn't expect to see you back here, ever, but especially not this soon."

Mr. Stiles glanced around. "Where is your lovely wife?"

"Umm, sir, I need a favor from you." Will quickly explained that he had no memory since the incident and would appreciate anything they could tell him about himself and his wife.

Mr. Stiles insisted he join them, and for the next hour, they explained everything to him.

"How did I end up separated from her? The Indians didn't say anything about a stagecoach or any women being involved in the fight I was in. Surely I wouldn't have come back this far for a fight after I made it home with her. You don't think she's hurt or kidnapped, do you?"

Mrs. Stiles offered a suggestion. "Mr. Gentry, why don't you see if the sheriff knows anything helpful? He's a good friend of yours, even vouching for your character before we took you seriously."

"Yes, I'll do that. I'll be by your office in the morning to get my information from you. Surely someone is looking for me, or perhaps worried about me, and I should send word I'm okay."

Will was relieved to find out so much information and hoped he would start remembering things on his own now. He walked to the sheriff's office, disappointed to find he had left for the night.

At least he knew his name and could look forward to knowing more after talking with the sheriff. Now, he had a growing concern for his wife, Sophie. Where was she? What had happened to her? Why and how were they separated?

The next morning he was eagerly greeted by the sheriff with a hearty handshake. "Will! Where have you been? We had a major manhunt going on for you! The judge and your ma are beside themselves."

Will hurried to explain, then stated his major concern. "I found out last night that I got married recently and somehow got separated from my wife. I've got to know if she's okay and what has happened to her."

The sheriff quickly eased Will's burden, telling him Sophie was okay. "Will, you and the men you were with kept the outlaws far from the stage. Since most of the men had rewards on them, it was decided to overtake them before they had the chance to get to the stage.

"Your 'friends' said you were adamant about it. But for now, we need to get word to Judge Gentry and your wife that you are alive and somewhat well."

Will nodded in appreciation. "Yeah, I guess I will write letters to follow the telegram. It's going to be strange writing to people I don't even remember, but I will explain as best I can."

The sheriff walked with Will to the telegraph office, as he told Will about his and Sophie's plan to visit his parents before settling down so far away.

"Then maybe I will continue with that plan. Maybe seeing my parents and homeplace will make me regain my senses."

Will looked at the sheriff mischievously. "Tell me, Tim, is my wife pretty?"

Tim chuckled and slapped Will on the back. "You did good, Will. That's all I have to say."

****

Sophie almost stopped, quickly deciding to continue on through the kitchen as if she hadn't heard anything. She let the cook know she was back as she hurried to her office and locked the door behind her.

"Lord, please help me. Please don't let who I thought I heard be real."

There was a knock on her door, followed by the cook's voice saying she needed to come quickly.

Sophie jerked the door open in alarm, gasping when she saw three men standing there, one holding the cook's arm.

The man turned the cook loose, telling her to get back to work and keep her mouth shut. Two men stood outside the door while the third man entered Sophie's office.

"Hello, my darling daughter. Why such an unpleasant look? Is that any way to greet your pa?"

Sophie's fear turned into fury. "I'll tell you how I should greet you!" She stepped forward and spat in his face.

He smiled cynically as he grabbed her arm and twisted it behind her back, pulling her back up against

92

himself before whispering in her ear. "I will be staying the winter with you, rekindling our relationship. Be nice so the people you care about don't start getting hurt."

She knew how ruthless this man was, and her first thoughts were of him having no hesitation about hurting her workers or her boys. Slowly, she nodded.

He released her. "Now, that's better. How about getting me and the boys a few rooms? Right now, we can make do with two, but before this little family reunion is over, we will need several more. Sure hope this place slows down during the winter where we can hope to have a bit of privacy."

"What do you want?" she asked while showing no fear. "Why are you here?"

"Let's just say I missed you."

"Let's not and just tell me the truth! Oh, I'm sorry, I forgot, you don't know how to tell the truth!"

He chuckled. "Now, Sophie, this is the truth. If you weren't my daughter, you wouldn't get by with that kind of talk. But seeing that I have missed you so, I will try to remember where you got that spirit from. Don't push me though. You know I don't tolerate disrespect or disobedience. This is your fair warning."

She started past him toward the door and he grabbed her arm.

"Where do you think you're going?"

She slung his hand from her arm and stared in his face. "I'm going to get you a room so you can take your stench out of my office!"

He backhanded her across the face. "I warned you, little girl. Now, let's see about a little respect, huh?"

Sophie held her face as she fought back tears. She walked past him and went toward the front desk of the hotel. Eyeing the available keys hanging on the wall, she selected the two rooms farthest away, upstairs and at the back.

Handing him the keys, she told him where the rooms were. "You should have privacy there. But let me give you a few warnings. I run a respectable business and I can't have anyone ruining it. I will have to remain here long after you're gone. I won't have anyone trying to turn this into a drinking, gambling, brothel.

"If you don't want the law around here getting suspicious of your activity, I expect you to comply."

"I understand your concern, dear daughter, but you seem to forget that I fear no lawman. For now, I will see if I can keep my men under control, just for you, just for now. I can't say how stir crazed they may get before the winter's over."

She walked back to the kitchen feeling completely demoralized. She had to get her thoughts under control and figure out how to keep her boys out of harm's way.

Trying to keep everything as normal as possible, she worked in the kitchen, staying busy while deep in thought and prayer.

It was almost time for the boys to come home from school when she walked through the dining room making sure everything was as it should be. She saw one of her pa's men sitting at the entrance between the dining room and the hotel lobby, pretending to read the paper as he kept an eye on everyone.

She walked past the hotel desk with hopes of meeting her boys and bringing them through the back door of the kitchen instead of the lobby. She didn't want her pa or his men to see them any sooner than necessary.

"Mrs. Collins," the desk clerk called. "You had a telegram delivered a few moments ago."

She thanked him as she took it and continued on her way out the door. Reaching the corner of the hotel, she watched for the boys as she opened the telegram. Her eyes went wide, then filled with tears.

Alive and well – letter following

She felt like shouting for joy. Relief flooded over her so strong, her knees almost buckled under. Then fear engulfed her. As much as she needed Will and wanted him with her, she couldn't bring anyone else into this dangerous situation. Her pa wouldn't hesitate much about inflicting pain and harm on her or her boys, but what he may do to Will was too horrible to imagine.

Suddenly, a hand reached around from behind her, snatching the telegram. She flew around to face the man who had been sitting, reading the paper.

Grabbing for the telegram, she gritted her teeth, demanding, "How dare you! Give me that immediately!"

The man held it high enough that she couldn't reach it and laughed. "Let's see what we have here. Boss wants to know all your comings and goings, which includes who you talk to and get mail and messages from."

He read the telegram. "How sweet. Who's it from?"

"I don't answer to you!" she huffed as she kicked him in the shin.

The man bent down to rub his shin with one hand, while reaching to grab her with the other, but she moved too fast and took off down the street toward the school.

What was she going to do? She was a prisoner in her own home. How could she protect her boys? She needed to get a message to someone, anyone, about what was going on, but she knew that anyone who got involved would be in great danger. If she could just divert the boys from coming home today, perhaps send them to the preacher for the night, she could figure something out. She would just say she was ill and hope he would just keep the boys and not come check on her.

Her hopes faded quickly as the man caught up with her, grabbing her arm. "That wasn't very nice. Now, let's start over. My name is Bill, and you need to get used to me being around. Don't give me reason to hurt you because I assure you, I won't think twice about it."

She shrugged off his hand. "Keep your hands off of me. I'll have you know that everyone in this town expects a certain behavior from me, watching me closely because I am widowed. If you don't want to draw unwanted attention, don't make me scream, because as you said, I assure you, I won't think twice about it."

She couldn't show any fear, or she would lose any control she may hope to gain.

The man looked at a loss for a moment as he continued to walk beside her. "Where do you think you're going?"

"I don't know. I wasn't going anywhere until you made me mad." She knew there was no way to get to the school and tell her boys to go to the preacher's for the night.

She sighed. "I guess I will go back home and get ready for the supper crowd." She resigned herself to the fact that her boys would soon become known to these men; there was no way around it.

Returning to the kitchen, she had to talk with the cook to smooth things out, keeping the woman from any danger. She explained that her pa had decided to pay an unexpected visit and would probably stay for the winter.

"We didn't part on good terms years ago, which is why we had a rough start. But everything will be okay. I am a bit embarrassed and would appreciate you keeping this to yourself."

The cook nodded, unconvinced. "Yes, ma'am, as you wish."

She walked toward the back door to watch for the boys. As she rounded the corner, there stood her pa.

Startled, she jumped, and her hand went to her throat. "What are you doing lurking around like that?"

He chuckled. "Just checking to see how much I can trust you. I like the way you handled your employee. As you know, I have to keep check on everything going on in my surroundings. That means all correspondence coming and going."

He pulled the telegram from his pocket. "Who is this from?"

She checked her tone before speaking, not wanting him riled before the boys came in.

"Not meaning any disrespect, but don't you have enough of your own business to be concerned with, without taking on my personal affairs? Do you intend to learn what it takes to run my business? How much sugar, flour, and coffee I order?

"I gave you a room, I will feed you while you're here, but we need to have some mutual respect."

He laughed. "No. You have to earn trust and respect. Now, who is the telegram from?"

She sighed. "I recently met a young woman named Carmen who was on her way to meet her husband to be. She was just letting me know that she finally finished her journey. I guess I will get the details in the letter she promised, which is no business of yours. She may say private things only a woman should read about."

"Hmm, well, you may be right." He scratched his chin. "I tell you what, I don't see any harm in you getting your private mail and bills and such, but not one message of any kind leaves here, even an order for sugar, without me knowing. I may change my mind, depending on how we get along."

That was the best she could hope for at this point. At least he was calm and looked as if he had bathed. Maybe she could figure out how to keep him calm and somewhat happy while he was here, hopefully with no one getting hurt.

Sophie turned toward the door as it opened, and the boys came in. They hugged her quickly and looked at the man.

"Who's he?" Gabe asked as he pointed.

Sophie corrected him. "Gabe, that is rude. You don't point, and you don't ask that way. You introduce yourself first, remember?"

Boss stood still, wearing a stunned look, not saying a word.

Gabe nodded his head and started again by extending his hand. "Good afternoon, sir. My name is Gabe Collins."

Boss took his hand and smiled. "Well, well, you don't say? It's nice to meet you, Gabe Collins. People call me Boss, but you can call me Grandpa."

He straightened and mumbled to Sophie. "I just may be able to trust you after all."

Sophie understood the threat completely.

Chapter 9

Will finished both letters and posted them, knowing he would probably reach his parents before the letter did.

His family celebrated with him privately when he arrived, trying not to overwhelm him.

Judge Gentry had already made arrangements for him to see a doctor, not knowing what he had been through, and was shocked to see him seemingly well but not knowing his own family.

His ma cried tears of joy and then sorrow as she hugged him often. She prepared all of his favorite foods and pampered him as much as he would allow.

Earl was the one who acted the most normal and actually helped break through the memory barrier with his teasing. Will followed him around the homeplace and helped with chores as Earl reminded him of teases, pranks, and secrets they had shared over the years.

Will began to remember some things from their childhood, even though it gave him a headache. He didn't want to stop remembering, but the ache was becoming a throb, and he asked for a break from talking for a while.

He actually walked to the right bedroom, which helped to boost his confidence, then he rested for a little while before he started pushing forward.

The next day, he rode to town accompanied by his entire family for his doctor's appointment. At the edge of town, he asked them to let him try to get his bearings and attempt to find the doctor on his own as they followed behind.

As his horse trotted into town, Will had glimpses of scenes run quickly through his mind. Going slowly by the sheriff's office, he felt a sense of bittersweet. He had been told he had been a sheriff here but didn't know why he had quit. He supposed it had something to do with falling in love with and marrying Sophie.

Without even concentrating, he pulled up in front of the doctor's as if it were a normal act. Feeling a bit better about things coming together, he dismounted and waited to help his ma from her buggy.

A little while later, the doctor concluded that Will was in great shape physically, trying to explain what little he knew about memory loss.

"In most cases I've heard of, it's just a temporary thing. With you already starting to remember, I hope it will return completely, very soon. You may experience headaches, dizziness, and perhaps even pass out as you begin to remember. It may come gradually, or it may come all at once when something jars your memory, perhaps a traumatic event."

He gave Will some medicine to ease his headaches as they left his office.

Meandering down the street, they pointed out places and told of events from the past. Will could remember the things from his childhood, but nothing as an adult...until he got to the saloon.

He stopped and broke into a sweat, swinging around and looking toward the spot where Mrs. Lindsay had been shot. "Something happened here. Tell me what happened here."

Judge Gentry put his hand on Will's shoulder as he told him about the incident that caused Will to give up his badge. After the explanation, Will began to remember.

"Seems as though something happened right before that. I had my mind on something else."

The judge finished telling him about Myra breaking up with him. "But son, that break up was for the best. You were never upset about the breakup, just about Mrs. Lindsay getting hurt."

"What happened after that?"

"Well, we aren't quite sure. You stayed gone a little over a year, drifting and doing odd jobs. You came home for a few weeks, then took off to marry Sophie. A week after you left here was when the fight happened, the same day you married Sophie."

Will nodded his head as his ma interrupted the conversation, suggesting they have lunch in the diner. She needed to talk to Will about Sophie, alone. Her husband didn't know, nor did he need to know all the details leading up to Will's decision to get married. She would tell him when they had some time alone.

Later, when Will was helping Earl with the chores, Will started asking about Sophie. Earl was a fountain of information.

"It would be best not to ask Father about her. He thinks she's too spirited and certainly doesn't agree with the way you and her got married."

"Spirited?" Will asked in amusement.

"Yeah. No one has ever spoken to the judge like she did. You were missing, and she was worried. He knew something about what had happened, and she was determined to find out.

"Of course, Father never told her what he knew, and he pretty much sent her on her way. I took her to the train station the next morning."

"So she feels abandoned by my family?"

"No. Ma made it clear that she accepted her as a daughter and would share any information she found out. Sophie invited her, and all of us to come visit any time. But she needed to get home to her boys. That's why she didn't fight with the judge anymore."

"Her boys?" Will swallowed hard.

"Yep, that's why she was looking for a husband in the first place, but you fell for her hook, line, and sinker, apparently."

Will shook his head. "Doesn't sound like I've thought clearly for a long time."

"Ma can explain it all better than I can. Her and Sophie hit it off with each other and spent more time together. All I know is when you left here to go meet her, you had already been in love with her for a month, saying you knew she was the woman the Lord had meant for you. You were determined to come back married."

"Earl, I feel another headache coming on. I'm going to ask you to stop talking now."

Earl chuckled as Will pulled out his bandana and wiped the sweat from his face and neck, even with the late September chill in the evening air.

****

Sophie saw an opportunity to turn things around a bit, perhaps gaining an advantage. Maybe she could even get her pa to let his guard down a bit. She hated to use her boys, but they were already caught in the middle, and her pa was going to be here through the winter, so she needed to make everything work as calmly as possible.

"Boys, go put your things away and get washed up for your snack," Sophie instructed.

"But Ma," Calvin looked up as he whined. "We have a grandpa! Can't we play with him for a while?"

"Boys, Grandpa is going to be here for a long time. There will be plenty of time for play. Right now, you do as I say."

105

Boss looked at her quizzically as the boys disappeared into the other room. "Two boys, huh? Any more surprises? I heard you were widowed, but is there a new husband or beau I need to be aware of?"

"No, I don't have the time or energy to find or take care of a man. A few have tried to win me, but I'm not interested."

"You expect me to believe you take care of a business and raise two boys without help?" Boss shook his head. "I'm not a fool. Now, out with it. Try the truth this time."

Sophie looked at him in mock hurt. "I'm telling the truth, but I didn't say I didn't have help; I said I don't have a man.

"The preacher and his wife have taken the boys under their wings as grandparents of sorts. The boys spent more time with them during the summer than with me. It gave me the time I needed to keep the business running during the busy time of year.

"Don't worry, Pa, you don't have to keep a close watch on my whereabouts. I stay too busy to get into mischief. I won't cause you trouble or concern."

"Good to know."

"Now, if you will excuse me? I have a lot to do. My evening routine can't be tampered with. You will either have to make yourself useful or stay out of my way so I can get everything done."

He grinned and motioned for her to go about her business. "I'll just stand back and see about this routine of yours."

Watching as Sophie helped the boys with their studies while the dining room was all but empty before supper, he soon became bored.

Every few minutes she would get up and stir a pot, put something in the oven, or take something out, then come back and help the boys some more.

"Can we go play with Grandpa now?" Calvin asked as he looked around and grinned at Boss.

"I don't know, boys. Grandpa may be too tired. He's had a big day."

"But he's been resting for a long time," Gabe declared. "Can we at least talk to him?"

Sophie looked at her pa and shrugged, waiting for his response.

Boss had been leaning back in a chair sipping coffee. He sat forward, set his cup down, and motioned for the boys.

They hurried to him as Sophie cringed. "Lord, please don't let him hurt my boys," she whispered as she stood, keeping a close watch on them.

Calvin immediately climbed up on Boss' lap and put his hands on his scraggly face. "Are you my real grandpa?" The boy spoke with so much hope and excitement in his voice, Boss actually had to smile.

"I sure am. What about that?"

Before she knew it, the boys had brought out a game and had Boss engrossed in it as they explained how to play. She watched them warily as she went about getting supper ready for her guests.

Her mind whirled as she thought about all of her employees coming in close contact with these men. Two girls worked the morning and lunch shift, along with cleaning hotel rooms, two other girls worked the supper shift, two men kept the hotel desk running seventeen hours a day, and the cook was there from before breakfast until right before supper. Sophie took over preparing supper when the cook left each evening.

Other than the cook, all of Sophie's girls were young and attractive, which concerned her with this lowlife being around.

Sophie made a mental note of which of them was most likely to see too much and perhaps cause trouble. If she could just keep everyone safe until the first big snow, she wouldn't have near as many people to worry about then. She would only have the cook, one waitress on each shift, and Sophie would take over the hotel desk herself; but that may be weeks away.

Constantly, in the back of her mind, was Will. She knew as soon as he came to town, which could be anytime now, he would make himself known to her, and to her pa and his men. If only she could get word to him.

At eight o'clock, she sent the boys to bed, locked the dining room door, and started cleaning up, just as if nothing was amiss.

Boss joined her in the kitchen. "I must say, this has been a right pleasant day. You have surprised me with how well you have chosen to take all of the changes."

She talked over her shoulder as she continued washing dishes. "I certainly don't understand why. I told you, this is my life. Nothing veers or changes much. I just look at this as having uninvited guests that took me by surprise. I really don't see where you have reason to be so cautious of me.

"I figure that if we keep everything as normal as possible, we just might get through this without incident. But with someone constantly watching every move I make, it causes other people to notice and makes me feel awkward."

She turned toward him and dried her hands. "I don't know why you're here. I don't know what you want. I would like to be able to extend the same courtesy to you and your men that I do to any of my guests, but without feeling like I'm a prisoner of some sort. What would I have to gain by…what? What exactly are you afraid I'll do? Tell someone you're here? You and your men are doing that yourselves by being so obvious. You stick out like sore thumbs.

"Who cares if you're here? Who would I tell and why?" She shook her head. "I just don't understand."

Suddenly her eyes went wide, and she gasped. "You're bringing trouble to our town? People are going to get hurt and possibly killed?"

He sat down and motioned for a cup of coffee. "No, nothing like that. I don't trust you, Sophie. I don't trust anyone. I have to watch my back every moment, which sometimes causes me to shoot before I have the chance to think. I've lived this way too many years, making enemies all along the way.

"I really just wanted a quiet place to bed down for the winter and not do anything for a change. I only brought two men with me, and that should tell you I'm not looking for trouble."

Sophie looked suspicious. "I don't believe you. You said that you needed two rooms for now but would need plenty more before this family reunion was over."

"Don't concern yourself with my business," he grinned slyly. "Just take one day at a time and everything will be fine."

"No, it won't. Not if you alarm every customer that comes in here."

He rubbed his chin. "Let me think on it. I've pushed and shoved my way around for so long, maybe it would be interesting to see how to be 'normal' for a change, just until this visit is over.

"But," he stood and pointed at her, looking gruff. "Don't be pulling anything on me. I will be watching you, just more discreetly."

He drank down his coffee. "Bill or Hardy will be outside your door all night, every night, just in case you might, umm, need something."

"Fine! But again I ask, why? What do you think I'm going to do? I'm certainly not going to leave you here and run from everything I have worked so hard for. What purpose would that serve, and where would I go?"

She picked up his empty cup and put it in the sink. "It just doesn't make sense. I'm going to bed. See you in the morning."

****

The next morning, Hardy was sitting outside her door and accompanied her to the kitchen to start her day. He sat in a corner where he could see yet not be noticeably staring at her.

After the boys left for school, she made her way to the dining room. She was surprised when she approached a table, finding Bill and her pa sitting there, clean shaven and wearing clean clothes.

"My! Isn't this a pleasant surprise? How does it feel to fit in for a change?"

Boss returned her smile. "I figure, you scratch my back and I'll scratch yours."

"Deal," Sophie nodded.

"I still don't trust you, Sophie."

"The feeling is very mutual, Pa."

****

Three days after Sophie received the telegram from Will, the letter he promised arrived. Bill had escorted her to run her errands, as always, with her walking steps ahead of him, pretending they didn't know each other.

"What kind of mail have you got there?" he asked as she passed by him on the boardwalk.

"None of your business. If Pa wants to see, he can ask me himself." She put the mail in her pocket and took off at a fast walk, greeting several people as they passed.

When Bill reported to Boss, he was surprised to find that Boss wasn't concerned with what came in, just adamant about knowing what went out.

Sophie thanked her pa politely and went to her office to attend to her business.

She opened all the mail and placed the unfolded letter among the bills and other correspondence, flipping through to read it while no one was interrupting her.

Will explained briefly about his ordeal and that he had no memory of her or his family. He was going to visit his family because they were close by and try to get more answers.

Be assured that I can't wait to meet you again. I will send a telegram announcing my arrival. Hopefully, it will be very soon.

Chapter 10

Will sent a telegram to Sophie announcing his arrival on Sunday. He had enjoyed the time with his family but was anxious to meet his wife again and hopefully regain the rest of his memory. So far, he could at least vaguely remember all of his years up until he left the sheriff's position. From that point, he had brief pictures flip through his mind that made no sense yet.

He saw himself in several tangles with men but figured that could be from his years of being a sheriff. Other times he saw rough looking men that seemed to be friends. He got glimpses of a hotel room, a church, and several other flashes, but nothing big enough to grasp.

Now, he wanted to remember the face of his wife, Sophie. Shaking his head and smiling, he could scarcely believe that he had married someone with two children.

He patted his horse as they rode along. "Well, boy, she must really be something." The horse snorted as if to agree, making Will chuckle as he urged him to pick up the pace.

Pulling into town about mid-morning, he rode down the main street taking in everything. Noticing there was only one hotel, he told his horse, "This must be the place."

He dismounted and walked to the door, noticing it wasn't open for business yet. Remembering it was Sunday, he realized the diner didn't open until lunch.

Glad to be off his horse after several hours of riding, he walked his horse to the livery to have him taken care of while waiting.

Arriving back at the diner a half hour later, he saw the door open from the inside as he stepped up on the porch. His heart felt as if it would beat out of his chest. He was getting ready to meet his wife…again. Her having two children, yet he still married her, let him know she had to be special.

Stepping inside a moment later, he saw a young woman walking away from the door, looking to be in a hurry to attend to two men sitting at a table. He supposed that the men must have entered through the hotel entrance because he sure hadn't seen them outside.

As the young woman turned from taking the men's order, Will stopped her. "Excuse me, ma'am," he spoke as he removed his hat.

She stopped and looked at him.

"Umm, are you Sophie?" What a dumb question, he thought. If she had been Sophie, wouldn't she have recognized him? Hopefully she would have shown some emotion about seeing him.

The young woman blushed. "No, sir. Mrs. Collins will be in soon."

"Thank you," he replied. Turning his hat in his hands, he made his way toward the hotel lobby, which separated the hotel and diner. His stomach was in knots, and he couldn't even think of eating.

Boss and Hardy were sitting where they could keep an eye on this man.

"Wonder what he wants with Sophie?" Boss asked quietly. "Apparently he doesn't know her from Adam. Wonder who he is and what his business is with her."

Boss took a closer look at Will. "Dressed too fancy for a cowpoke. Probably a businessman or lawyer or something."

He kept watch on the man even as his food was set in front of him and he began to eat.

Will glanced at the men a few times as he felt their eyes on him. He shifted uncomfortably and began to sweat. Waiting was making him nervous enough without being stared at. He took out his bandana and wiped his face quickly.

Boss snickered. "Whoever he is, he seems a mite nervous about meeting Sophie. This may be entertaining."

Hearing the boys beginning to chatter from the kitchen, Boss knew Sophie would soon be coming to the dining room after getting the boys settled for their lunch in the kitchen. A few minutes later, he saw her appear at the kitchen door. He set his fork down and sat back to watch.

Will heard voices of children in the kitchen and hoped that meant Sophie wasn't too far off. He waited nervously and paced slowly, trying to calm his breathing and his heart.

Suddenly, she came through the door, and he recognized her immediately. She didn't see him until he rushed toward her, embracing her tightly and locking her into a passionate kiss.

Thinking as quickly as possible, she kept herself from embracing him in return, finding that to be one of the hardest things she had ever had to do.

When he released her, she quickly whispered, "Trust me, please."

She slapped him across the face. "How dare you! And right in front of my pa!"

Will stood there dumbfounded as memories flooded his mind along with the confusion. That was when he noticed that three men were standing around him, all with guns pointed at him.

"What's going on here?" Boss growled.

Sophie quickly jumped in front of Will, motioning for everyone to calm down. "Wait! I think I know what this is all about. Please, put your guns away, and don't alarm my customers."

Boss nodded slowly to his men. "This better be good. Some stranger come in here and take such liberties. He didn't even know who you were. Asked your waitress if she was Sophie."

Sophie turned to Will. "Is your name Will? Carmen sent you, didn't she?" She started nodding, hoping Will would follow her lead, and he did.

Sophie started to chuckle and put her hand on Will's arm, acting so relieved. "Carmen sent word you were coming but I never thought you would be so brazen!"

"Please, come have a seat." She motioned for Will to follow her.

"Pa, I've got this under control, please just go back and finish your meal."

"No." He sounded gruff and firm. "I will join you. Something isn't right about this whole thing, and I want to know what's going on." He looked at Sophie as if he could see right through her.

Sophie shrugged nonchalantly. "As you wish."

The three sat down in the lobby, while Hardy and Bill stayed close.

Will hadn't uttered a sound, waiting to follow Sophie's lead. He had to pay close attention because she seemed to be trying to send him a message, a warning.

"Pa, let me tell you what this is all about first, then we can talk. You remember I told you about traveling this summer with a young woman named Carmen? She was on her way to meet her new husband?"

Boss nodded even though his hackles were still up. "I remember."

"Well, this is her brother, Will Garner. She wrote to him about me and must have told him more than she admitted." She looked shyly at Will.

"Anyway, I got a letter from her a few days ago saying her brother was coming out to visit her and might stop by to meet me on his way through. I just had no idea it would be so soon."

She looked at Will in disappointment. "Looks like another rude man. Between not informing me of your arrival, and greeting me in such a way, I'm afraid you have lessened your chances with me already."

Will cleared his throat. "I'm so sorry, Mrs. Collins. I suppose I had my hopes up so high by what Carmen told me about you, and then when I saw such beauty…I guess I took leave of my senses. I assure you, I have never done anything like that before. Please forgive me, ma'am."

"Good way to come up dead," Boss mumbled.

Sophie stood. "Are we finished here?" She looked at both of them.

Will stood. Bill and Hardy put their hands on their guns and stepped forward.

"Mrs. Collins, please. I would like another chance to at least speak with you. I promise to be an absolute gentleman. Besides, I need a room for a few days."

Sophie looked sad. It was all she could do to contain herself. "There is a boarding house down the street. You certainly can't stay here; it wouldn't be decent. You can take your meals here, and I will consider your request."

She went back to the kitchen with her pa not far behind, while Bill and Hardy motioned for Will to leave.

Now his head was really spinning and aching. He had to think…He had to remember everything she had told him when they first met and everything she said today. Something was terribly wrong. She was in danger, or she would have never gone through such pains to make up a story like that and give him a different name.

He got a room at the boarding house and rested on the bed, trying to get rid of his headache. Needing to think clearly, he didn't dare take any of the medicine the doctor gave him.

His thoughts went to the only time that he and Sophie had really talked. Remembering that she had been widowed and she had two boys, he felt on the verge of remembering something, but it wouldn't come.

He went to the diner for supper a bit early, famished from not eating since his breakfast of jerky, and he hoped to get there before the supper crowd came in.

Sophie peeked in the dining room several times checking on her customers, always catching his eye and slightly shaking her head at him.

Will saw one of the goons with guns sitting in the lobby, peering over the newspaper, watching every move. What in the world was going on? She almost seemed to be a prisoner in her own hotel.

He put his elbows on the table and his face in his hands as he massaged his temples for a moment. *"Her pa,"* he thought. *"What did she tell me about her pa? He was a sheriff, no, her deceased husband was a sheriff. Her pa was…"* he blew out a sigh. "I don't remember."

Finishing his meal, he put his money on the table and left, tipping his head to the goon on his way out.

Sophie's heart sank as she watched him leave. This wasn't the way it was supposed to be, but to keep him out of harm's way, it was the way it had to be.

"So, dear daughter, what are the young man's chances?" Boss laughed as he sat at the table in the kitchen while she washed dishes.

"Hmph," she retorted. "What do you think? A little too brazen to suit me."

"I like a brave man who knows what he wants and goes after it." Boss propped his feet on the table.

"Yes, I suppose you would," she snapped sarcastically. She turned and gasped. "Speaking of brave! You are brave or stupid to put your feet on my clean table like that!" She took his feet and swung them to the floor.

"I already have guests and two boys I have to clean up after. I would appreciate you not making my job any harder!"

"Well, excuse me!" he snipped at her. "Looks as though you have a lot of your spitfire ma in you that I had forgotten about."

She smiled. "Yes, I guess I do. Perhaps you should remember that."

Sitting down to join him with a cup of coffee, she worked on him a bit more. "Pa, life shouldn't be this hard. It seems as though it's always been so hard."

Boss looked around. "I don't know, you look like you're pretty well off to me."

She looked at him. "Don't get me wrong, I'm thankful and blessed to have what I do, but it's not like it was handed to me, and I have to work hard every day to keep it.

"But, I guess I was thinking more about family life. Growing up without a ma was hard, especially with me being the only girl, I suppose. Then, life with you was hard. When you were home, it seemed you were always mad, drunk, and demanding. But when you were gone, life was still hard because my brothers were mean, mad, demanding, and sometimes as they got older, drunk.

"I always dreamed of a life with a perfect little family of my own." She sighed. "There for a while, I almost had it. But for some reason, perfection was just beyond my grasp."

Boss leaned forward, looking for a moment like he really cared. "Sophie, I'm not the one to be telling this sentimental tripe to. I don't have a heart. I have no compassion, no patience, no feelings."

Sophie's eyes filled with tears. "Yes, I guess I forgot who I was speaking to. I guess I hoped you had changed. Maybe I should keep the boys away from you so you don't end up losing your patience with them. I don't want them to ever know how mean and cruel you can be."

"That may be a good idea. That little Calvin is hard not to get attached to. Both the boys are cute kids, but I don't need to be getting a soft spot. It always causes trouble. I can find plenty of that on my own."

"Well then, either you need to stay in your room more often, or I need to speak with the preacher about them spending more time with him."

Boss nodded. "I'll spend more time in my room while they're up and about. Don't need no preacher poking around here getting in our business."

He stood and said goodnight as he went through the door.

She had thought for a moment that he was beginning to soften. How could he be so heartless?

Chapter 11

Will lay awake in his bed for a long time, thinking and praying. Finally, he drifted off to sleep, having a mix of good and bad dreams. When he awoke, the sky was just beginning to show a little light.

He looked in the mirror and determined that he liked this clean look so much more than what he looked like a few weeks earlier.

A memory came flooding back. "I was a bounty hunter. I remember now. That's why I took that man in for a reward. That's the life I was living after I gave up my badge. But…something changed. I wasn't a bounty hunter when I met Sophie, was I?"

He shook his head to clear it. "I need to focus on what's going on in that hotel. Sophie is in danger. Who are those men with her pa? What…oh no! She said her pa was an outlaw, and her husband was the sheriff who rescued her from him. She's in danger for sure and trying to keep me out of it, trying to handle it on her own. I've got to think and figure something out."

Before it got any lighter outside, he got dressed and went quickly to the sheriff's office. He needed to get a look at the wanted posters.

He asked to speak with the sheriff.

"We haven't had a full-time sheriff for a while now, mister, but if you have trouble, we can handle it."

Will explained that he used to be a sheriff and wanted to take some time to look over some wanted posters. The deputy was very accommodating and led him to a back room, leaving him with a stack of wanted posters, and telling him to take his time.

As Will went through the stack, he remembered his fellow bounty hunters. They were a rough bunch and stayed to themselves, but he was sure he could find them. Suddenly his mind was clearer than it had been in months.

Then he saw it. A picture of a man, who, if he could erase the beard from the picture, was sure it was Sophie's pa. Those mean eyes were undeniable.

"Denny," he mumbled. "The gang we tried to catch so many times. The ones we fought to keep from the stage. The ones at the hotel weren't there that day.

"I'm going to need help. Sophie needs help."

****

Sophie had stayed up half the night writing as small and clearly as she could on a napkin. She hoped that at some point, she could slip it to Will. It explained everything she knew and an apology for slapping him.

She was greeted by a clean and somewhat cheerful Bill this morning instead of Hardy.

"I need to speak with you about something, or should I say, someone." Bill smiled crookedly as he followed her into the kitchen.

She went about getting everything done as usual as he followed her around the kitchen, speaking quietly.

"Tell me more about Sissy," he almost whispered.

"Sissy?" She turned to him with wide eyes. "My waitress, Sissy?"

He smiled and nodded. "She seems a lot more friendly than the others, and she sure is a pretty thing."

"No! I will not have you drooling over my girls!" She lowered her voice and pulled him toward the back door. "I won't have you or anyone putting her life in danger, which is exactly what will happen if you start making eyes at her."

"I wasn't exactly asking your permission. I was asking for information."

"I will speak to my pa about this. This was not part of the agreement! You stay away from my girls!" She spun on her heel and got back to work getting the boys' breakfast prepared.

Boss lumbered into the kitchen after the boys left for school.

Sophie greeted him with, "I hope you're proud of yourself. The boys were asking about you. Guess it's better now than after they get too attached."

"Well, good morning to you as well. I see you didn't sleep well."

"I slept just fine, thank you, and was in a fine mood until Bill started talking about one of my waitresses. I can't have him pulling anyone into a dangerous situation."

"Dangerous situation," he scoffed as he scooped a forkful of eggs into his mouth. "There ain't no dangerous situation. I'm just taking a vacation, remember?"

"Then why do I feel like a prisoner?"

He looked at her seriously. "Because you owe me. I won't tolerate your betrayal again. I don't trust you because I know you hate me."

Sophie's heart stopped. "I what? I betrayed you? I owe you?" Her face turned red with fury.

She sat down as close as she could get to him and got right in his face. With gritted teeth, she spoke as quietly as she could. "You let that man…hurt me. What was I supposed to do? Stay and let it happen again?"

Boss slammed his fist on the table, jumped up, and walked out the kitchen door into the alley.

Sophie followed him, knowing she was putting herself in danger of, at the very least, being slapped, but not caring at that moment.

Boss turned and looked at her. "I wasn't there! I didn't know until much later, and I will have you know, that man paid with his life for what he did, very slowly and painfully. And what thanks did I get for correcting the problem? You turned me in to that sheriff that you loved so much!

"Yes, I was a bad father. I was mean, wicked, and a lot of other things, but I wasn't an outlaw until you betrayed me. You put me on the wanted posters and caused me to be on the run for the rest of my life!"

"Don't you dare blame your wicked life on me! I saw you do unspeakable things to men and women as far back as I can remember."

"Oh really? Maybe you just saw half the story, little girl. Yes, I was mean, especially when I was drinking, but I never hurt anyone until they cheated me or stole from me. They all had it coming to them, until you forced me to leave my home and everything behind. I took your brothers because they were my boys, and you caused them to live the life of crime along with me.

"So, if I make your life a bit uncomfortable for the next few months, so be it. You've got that coming to you and a whole lot more! Just wait until your brothers join us for the reunion. They can't wait to see you."

In a matter of seconds, Sophie went from furious to fearful. Is that what they all truly believed, that she was to blame for their life of crime? Was she?

"No. Don't you pin this on me. If you had just stayed and told the judge what happened, backed my story up, it would have all been over with. You made your own choice to live a wicked life of crime.

"My husband went to the judge in your defense. He was the only one I had to count on, and yes, I guess because I was so young, it made me fall in love with him, or so I thought. When you left, you left me with a life of misery, confusion, and loneliness. I was a child, and as mean as you were sometimes, I still loved you. You were my pa!" Sophie broke into a sob, turning quickly and running back through the kitchen, to her office, slamming the door behind her.

Boss was so mad and upset, he needed to take a walk to cool down. He needed to think. He was trying his best not to have any compassion, emotions, or the slightest feelings for his daughter and his grandsons, yet was beginning to. He had done nothing but hate for so long, he didn't know how to act any other way.

For the first time in years, he took off walking by himself, without any of his men guarding him, not thinking about it or caring.

****

Will was walking to the diner for breakfast when he heard what sounded like an argument going on in the alley. He peeked around the corner and saw Sophie having it out with her pa. Hearing more than he wished he had, he stood still until it was over.

Peeking around the corner again, he saw Boss approaching, with none of his men in sight. He pulled his gun and waited.

As soon as Boss rounded the corner, Will stuck his gun in his ribs and grabbed his arm. "You are under arrest, and if you make one sound or move wrong, I promise it will be your last.

He walked Boss down the few doors to the sheriff's office, announcing that he had a prisoner.

"I can't share who he is yet, but he has paper on him. It would be too dangerous to let word get out about this, so don't let anyone know, and I mean anyone."

Will told the deputy to wire for the U.S. Marshal to come pick up some outlaws and bring plenty of armed escorts.

Will dug some money out of his pocket. "Here, stop at the diner and get us some breakfast, on me. But I'm serious, don't breathe a word about this, or several people will be in danger."

When the deputy returned, Will shared that there were at least two more outlaws from this gang, holed up in the hotel, keeping Mrs. Collins prisoner.

"They are going to miss their leader and things may get dangerous. I need to get to work before Mrs. Collins' boys get out of school."

Will instructed the deputy to keep the door locked constantly, not letting anyone in until the U.S. Marshal arrived, which could be days. Then he walked down the street to the diner.

****

"I don't know where he is, Bill," Sophie snapped. "I'm certainly not hiding him from you, and he is NOT my responsibility."

Bill was tired of her attitude and worried about Boss. "You better hope nothing happens to him. He's the only reason I put up with your sassy mouth."

"Well, I guess I should feel so lucky," she oozed with sarcasm as she turned toward the dining room.

Will had just come in and sat at a table near the lobby. He smiled at Sophie and tipped his head, shocked when she made a straight line toward him, with one of the goons not too far behind.

"Hello, Will," she smiled. "You just came in so, perhaps you could help us."

"Sure, if I can."

Sophie looked over her shoulder at Bill. "Did you happen to see my pa in town anywhere?"

"Well, yes. As a matter of fact, I even spoke to him. He was just down the street a bit."

"There, Bill, go find him."

Bill motioned for her to follow him. When they got back to the lobby, he gave her a quiet, stern warning. "Don't do anything stupid. Don't you run off."

"Just where would I go, Bill? This is my home and my business. Either stay and watch me, or go find my pa. Either way, I will be right here doing the same thing I always do. Go wake Hardy up to watch me."

He looked at her and shook his finger, then turned and went out the door.

She made sure he went past the window, then quickly went to Will.

"Will, I'm so sorry," she handed him the napkin quickly. "Hide this and read it later. It explains everything."

"Where's the other goon?"

"Sleeping, why?"

"When will he be up?"

"Probably another hour or two. He had night watch again."

"I'll be back." He jumped up quickly and left.

In less than an hour, Will was back with a deputy, asking that Sophie make sure the stairway stayed clear of guests until they were finished.

She gave him the spare key to the room Hardy was in and prayed as the men climbed the stairs.

After hearing a scuffle, they came back down with Hardy in shackles. They took him through the back alley to the sheriff's office and locked him in a separate cell from Boss and Bill.

Another deputy came in with a telegram saying the U.S. Marshal would arrive in four days. Will wasn't happy with that. If anyone found out about these arrests, the entire town would be in danger.

He thought and prayed, then sent out a few telegrams. Before he left the office, he made sure to warn about the importance of secrecy.

Before he returned to the sheriff's office, he made a quick stop by the diner. He didn't see Sophie in the lobby or dining room and made his way to the kitchen.

She smiled when she saw him and motioned toward her office, leading the way, and closing the door behind them.

He took her in his arms and held her close. "I love you, Mrs. Gentry. Your nightmare is over."

She eased her arms up around his neck and initiated the sweetest kiss ever.

When he pulled his lips from hers, he apologetically said, "I have to hurry back, and I will be on guard duty for a few days. After that, I'm all yours."

"I look forward to that."

He gave her one more quick kiss and left.

****

Late the next afternoon, three scraggly looking men rode into town, going straight to the sheriff's office. They knocked on the locked door and called out to Will.

"Hey, guys. Good to see you again." Will pointed to the cells and filled his 'friends' in on what was happening.

"The rest of the gang are supposed to show up sometime before spring, for what Boss called a reunion. How do you feel about holing up right here for the winter? Looks like it may be worth it."

One of the men spoke up, "You mean, Sonny and Junior's gangs are supposed to meet up here?"

"Yep."

"You're talking about twelve to twenty more men. We need more help."

"Yeah," Will smiled. "I already have them on the way. So, what do you say? Help me guard these men until the Marshal gets here, then have first-class accommodations for the winter, not to mention the reward on all the men we catch."

"Or kill," another man spoke with a deep voice. "They're easier to haul in dead."

Will knew this was a rough bunch, but he needed help and these men were loyal, at least to collect bounties. "Yeah, whatever it takes to keep this town safe. That is my main concern."

"Since when?" a man asked with a smirk.

"Since I'm married and have a family living here."

The men guffawed and backslapped Will.

****

Having all the men settled and instructions given on shifts to guard the prisoners, two men stayed with a deputy, while Will and the other bounty hunter went to the hotel for the night.

It had been over three months since Will and Sophie had taken their vows, and finally, they were together, in love, yet still practically strangers.

He held her close as she lay in his arms that night, with her head against his chest as his heart raced.

"Will? Are you happy?"

He kissed the top of her head. "Very. And you?"

She nodded her head. "I just wish this moment didn't have to end, but I know you need some sleep. Your room is right next door."

"What?" he chuckled.

She looked up at him. "I know you need your own room, and I understand."

"Sophie," he tipped her chin up. "I don't know what you're talking about. I intend to have you sleep by my side every night for the rest of my life."

She smiled. "Really?"

"Yes, now tell me why you would think otherwise."

"Well, my first husband always said we needed to sleep separately because he needed his sleep."

"Oh no, no. That's not how this works." He held her tighter. "I seem to remember thinking that you hadn't ever experienced romance, but sweetheart, I'm going to show you, and I think you will like it.

"And it goes so much deeper than physical. I will show you so much romance that it will go all the way to your soul, where you carry it with you every moment of the day."

She shivered with excitement as he took her in his arms and kissed her passionately.

Chapter 12

Sophie asked Will to be discreet until they could talk to the boys after school, so he slipped out and went to the sheriff's office before they came down for breakfast.

He was one happy man, especially when he found everything to be fine with the prisoners. They changed men on watch and settled in for the day.

Shortly after noon, four more men Will had sent for arrived. A couple of them really looked and acted rough, and he started having second thoughts about having them stick around all winter, but they could silently sneak up on someone and pull a blade, quicker than most men could pull off one shot.

He left them on watch and went to take care of some quick business, first with his wife, then hopefully, he would be busy with construction.

Explaining the situation to Sophie, she quickly agreed to move all of her things out of the office and let Will turn it into a room with several bunks for the men. He felt good about having someone close to that back door in the alley also.

Will and a couple of other men were busy constructing the bunks when the boys came home from school. Sophie asked if he could join her, and they sat down with the two boys.

"Gabe, Calvin, this is Will. He is going to be staying with us and is a very special man."

Gabe looked him over intensely. "What are you special at?"

Will smiled and cleared his throat. "Well, let's see. I can skip a rock across a lake, I'm a champion at shooting marbles, I can make the sound of several birds and some other animals, and I can eat a whole apple pie at one time and not get sick from it."

Calvin's eyes got big. "Yep, you're special!"

Gabe wasn't convinced. "But can you catch a frog or a lizard? Do you know how to fish, hunt, and shoot a gun? Can you do math?"

Will rubbed his chin. "I have to admit, I haven't caught a frog or a lizard in a long time. You may have to help me with that. But yes, I know how to fish, hunt, and shoot a gun, and I know a bit about math. Why do you ask?"

Gabe shrugged. "I was supposed to take one of my friends a frog or a lizard last week, but Ma wouldn't let us go outside. We had to stay inside with Grandpa and his friends. Some of the boys at school talk about going fishing and hunting, and it sounds like fun, but we've never got to do that. And…" he looked sheepish. "I got a bad grade on my math and need some help with it. Ma has been busy lately and Grandpa didn't know how to help me."

"I see. Well, I think we can take care of all that, if your ma says it's okay, but not all at once. Sounds like the math and frog or lizard are most important right now."

Gabe smiled. "Really? Yeah, I guess you are special."

"Boys," Sophie smiled as she took Will's hand. "Will is your new pa, and he is going to be so good to all of us."

Calvin looked concerned. "He won't be grumpy like Grandpa?"

Will reached over and tickled Calvin as he pulled him on his lap. "Me? Be grumpy? Never!"

Calvin laughed and wiggled as Will reached for Gabe and pulled him close, kissing both on the top of their head. He winked at Sophie, who sat beside him, beaming with joy.

"Come on! We have a frog or lizard to catch. Do you know a good place to find some?" Will stood and motioned them toward the door. They left in a flurry of chatter. A moment later he returned, quickly kissing her and running back out to catch up with the boys...his boys.

****

When the U.S. Marshal and his men arrived, they had no idea who the prisoners were, but because of Will's reputation, and that of his father, they took him seriously. Arrangements were made to transport the men to prison by private rail car, still not releasing their identities to anyone.

Will was relieved when the men finally left town, now, he needed to get busy preparing for Sophie's other relatives. The deputy introduced Will to the mayor and sang high praises to him.

The men talked about the threat of things to come, with the mayor taking Will's concerns very seriously.

"How can I help you, Mr. Gentry? What do you and your men need?"

"Sir, I think it would be beneficial to build a tall lookout tower, without letting everyone know what's going on yet. There is no need for people to panic, and we really don't want word to get out about our plan, somehow warning the outlaws. For that reason, my men and I are the only ones who know the names of the men that just left here, and the ones on their way.

"We have no idea when they'll be arriving, so we need to work quickly. After the tower is built, if you would call a town meeting to explain a plan of emergency for everyone, then we can hopefully get everyone prepared."

The mayor nodded. "I will see to it you have everything you need. But I would like the chance to speak with you about something. You may need time to think about it, so if we could discuss it now?"

"Yes, sir. What can I help you with?"

"Mr. Gentry, you are young, strong, have experience as a sheriff, seem to be a born leader, and possess humility and integrity. That is just what we need here as a sheriff. I would like for you to consider the position."

Will looked away, slightly embarrassed. "Sir, thank you for those kind words, but I am so undeserving. I am no longer anything but a despicable bounty hunter."

"That's not the person I have heard of, and certainly not the one that is sitting here in front of me now, trying to protect this entire town. Bounty hunters are only interested in collecting bounty; that's not who you are."

Will stood. "Thank you, sir. I have to get busy." He shook the mayor's hand and left.

****

For the next ten days, Will and his crew of seven men, constructed a tall tower, standing twice as high as any buildings and trees near town. With a spyglass, you could see movement for several miles in most directions.

Satisfied with the finished product, the men sat down to supper together to discuss their thoughts about how to protect the people of the town. Sophie was brought in on the discussion after the boys went to bed, to let them know what townspeople would be beneficial and reliable.

Everything was planned to perfection, with alternate plans according to the time of day it may go into effect. Now, it was time to alert, not alarm, the people of the town.

Will had told Sophie about the offer from the mayor. At first, she was honored to think that her husband was so well liked and respected. Then the reality of the danger that came with that position weighed heavy on her. As she watched her husband during his planning, she realized just how caring and protective he truly was, not just of his family, but for everyone. That was the kind of man this town, these good people, needed.

Will bathed and dressed for the meeting, going over everything he was going to say. He had papers full of notes to guide him, but this kind of thing always made him nervous.

He chuckled as he looked in the mirror with Sophie standing behind him. "Why is it that I get so nervous in a room full of good, law-abiding citizens, yet in the middle of a gunfight, I'm calm?"

"Maybe because you feel responsible for protecting these people and need to make sure you don't let them down. While in a gunfight you are taking action against the ones trying to harm them."

He turned, taking her in his arms, kissing her gently. "I love you, Sophie."

"And I love you, Will." She paused for a moment. "You told me once that you thought being a lawman ran in your blood. I believe you. You have a natural instinct to protect not just your family, but everyone in your surroundings. I think you should take the mayor's offer."

He set her back from himself with his mouth gaped. "Sophie, that's not what we agreed on. You have this hotel and diner that you needed my help with, along with becoming an active father to our sons. There isn't enough time in a day to do that and be a sheriff, or really to hold any other job."

She smiled. "I disagree. You have been putting in so much time for the last few weeks preparing for the arrival of trouble, yet you still found time to take the boys fishing, help with their studies, and keep me happy." She winked at him.

"The way I see it, this is your purpose in life. Most men don't see as clear a path as what you've been given. I don't think you will feel totally happy being a full-time handyman because you would have missed your true calling. Besides, the extra money you make can help pay someone to do repairs when needed."

He wrapped his arms back around her. "You've got it all figured out, don't you?"

She nodded against his chest. "Although it's a dangerous job at times, and I know I will worry about you, I've never known a man to be so cut out for being a sheriff as you."

"I'll pray and think about it some more then. Now, let's get going."

The meeting went fairly well, especially after the people realized that the rough looking bunch in the room were there to protect them, not hurt them. The mayor introduced them and started the meeting, stating the purpose and urgency of it.

After gasps and a few tears from the ladies as they wrapped their children tighter against themselves, the mayor turned it over to Will.

Will had such a winning way about him, everyone calmed almost immediately. He motioned for Sophie to hand out the papers he had printed, telling the different plans according to the time of day it may happen.

"In case this happens during the school day, I need some volunteers to help the teacher move the children to the cellar of the church. I need some men to help move any horses from the street and out of the livery, taking them to Mr. Young's pasture."

The list went on for a long time, with everyone volunteering to do their part.

A man stood up in the back. "Where do you need us to be posted to help with the fight after we move the horses?"

Will was stunned momentarily, not completely understanding the man's question. "Umm, no, you just need to stay clear and let us take care of this."

"Sorry to dispute you, Mr. Gentry, but we aren't ones to sit back and not help protect our own."

Several men stood and agreed. Will looked at his men and shrugged before speaking. "I don't like to get civilians involved in such things. We are trained and have lots of experience dealing with these types of outlaws."

"I understand that, sir, but they are bringing this fight to our town, and that makes my blood boil. I'm fighting mad and insist on helping protect my own. What kind of men would we be if we stood back and did nothing?"

Will wanted to say that they would be alive and that had to count for something, but he knew how it felt to protect your loved ones.

"I understand. Anyone interested in taking up arms against these men, see me right after the meeting. But let it be known, I need lots more men protecting the women, children, horses, and property on the outskirts of town, just in case they don't all come in together."

He turned the meeting back over to the mayor and sat down beside Sophie.

"Ladies and gentlemen, if you would please allow me about five minutes? Let's take a short break, then we will get back to the actual business at hand."

Everyone started filing out of the church as the mayor rushed to Will and Sophie. "Mr. Gentry, may I speak with you?"

Sophie watched as they moved out of hearing distance. Whatever was being said looked to be agreeable with both men. When Will returned to her, he didn't say anything, and she didn't ask.

The mayor brought the meeting back to order. "We have several loud bells set out to be rung when the time comes. Before that time, we will have several practices, making sure that everyone knows what to do and where to go.

"But before we get into all of that, while I have the majority of you in town, I would like to take a vote on appointing a new sheriff. We have been without a permanent sheriff for way too long.

"I have found a man with integrity and plenty of experience as a sheriff that would be perfect for us. He cares about our community and the welfare of everyone in it. In the short time he has been with us, I think he has proven himself worthy. He has just given his permission to be considered.

"Could I have a show of hands of people in favor of Will Gentry being our new sheriff starting immediately?"

Will didn't dare to look around.

The mayor chuckled, "Well, Mr. Gentry, umm, I mean, Sheriff, looks as though you had pretty close to a unanimous vote!"

Applause erupted before the mayor could get back to the business at hand. Sophie laid her head on his shoulder and whispered how proud she was of him.

Chapter 13

Over the next week, everyone participated in getting everything prepared. Food and water were put in cellars in case of a longer stay than anticipated, the drill was practiced at all times of the day and night, and the volunteers had their posts assigned. Will and his men were well pleased.

Snow began to fall, which made life harder on everyone, but it kept more people off the streets and out of harm's way.

Will climbed to the top of the tower and greeted the two men there. "Well, boys, seems to me, if they plan on getting here before the spring thaw, they should be here soon. Everything will be impassable before much longer."

One of the men that went by the name Buffalo, grunted and responded gruffly. "My knives are about to rust from not being used. I'm getting kinda itchy myself."

Will looked at the man and was glad they were on the same side. Buffalo looked like a buffalo, standing about six foot six inches, weighing at least three hundred pounds, dressed warmly in a coat, boots, gloves, and hat, all made from buffalo.

The other man standing watch didn't look much friendlier, speaking with a surly voice. "My trigger finger is itchin' like crazy. Buff wants hand-to-hand combat; I like getting them in my crosshairs." He chuckled with an evil sound.

"Sophie will have a good, hot breakfast for you when you come in." Will turned to leave.

"I'll take mine to go," Buffalo responded almost cheerfully as he looked through his spyglass and pointed.

Everyone took a spyglass and looked in the same direction. Way off in the distance, they saw a glimmer of a campfire.

"I ain't waiting for them to bring the party to me," Buffalo smiled.

Will wasn't about to try to stop him. Buffalo was as stealth and stout as they came. "I'll go rustle up some breakfast for you and send someone else up here to relieve you."

Buffalo nodded, never taking his eyes off the campfire, and never losing that cynical smile. "Tell Manny it's time to dance. You be watching for the signal."

Will alerted the rest of his men, but no one else until they knew for sure. They didn't want to put out any false alarms.

****

"Sure will be nice to sleep in a bed tonight," Junior grumbled as he slurped the last swig of coffee. "Tired of hearing all that snoring."

He pulled his coat tighter and rubbed his hands over the fire. "Yeah, it's' going to be nice to be out of this weather, staying warm, eating good, and of course, all the benefits of being with family." He laughed. "May even see a few of my old friends from way back. Yes, what a reunion it will be."

He started barking orders for his eight men to get camp broke and the horses ready.

An hour later, they were packed up, ready to go. Junior looked around.

"We got some missing. We don't have time for anyone lagging behind. Who's missing?"

"I think that whining baby we brought along with us must have finally talked Doug into pulling out with him. I saw tracks headed back the other way."

Junior swore under his breath. "So be it. Good riddance! Let's go."

Manny watched them pass below him as he perched up in a tree, camouflaged and still as a statue. As soon as they were down the trail a bit, he set an arrow on fire and shot it up in the air to alert the town, keeping it behind and unnoticed by the outlaws.

Buffalo joined him a few minutes later, with one prisoner squirming and the other one no longer breathing. They stayed within the tree line, out of sight, but close enough to see every move.

****

Will was on the ground waiting for news from the men in the tower. Soon he was scrambling to ring the bell before the outlaws got close enough to hear it.

He was proud of the way everyone scurried to do what they had been trained to do. Everything was going as planned until one of the men called from the tower.

"Sheriff! We got trouble!"

Will climbed to the top of the tower in record time, taking the spyglass, looking in the direction the man pointed.

The gang Buffalo and Manny had taken off after, were coming from the South. Here was another gang coming from the West.

"Well, I wish we could have handled them one group at a time, but we knew this could happen. We're as prepared as we know to be."

The man pointed toward the east. "But we weren't expecting that."

Will swung around toward the East and focused on a late season wagon train heading their direction. His immediate thought was to warn these people that he had just become responsible for before they rode right into an ambush.

He needed every available man where they were assigned to be, with no one out in the open traveling toward that wagon train.

Will sighed. "I need someone to go tell them to stay put until we come get them." He put the spyglass down and asked who would be the best man for the job.

"I can do it!" Duff spoke up enthusiastically. "I have a white horse that won't be noticed with all the snow. If I can get someone to trade me a lighter colored coat, I can warn them and be back in no time."

"Go! Tell Sophie to give you my light duster to wear over your coat."

Duff took off with Will giving one last look at all the positions of their incoming company, before going to check on everything and everyone.

He walked down the empty street, seeing several men on rooftops and groups hidden at each end of the main street.

Four horses were tied in front of the general store, and a wagon was parked just past them, making it look as if there was some business going on. He checked several doors, making sure all were locked, then went to check the cellar of the church.

All the children were fine, and the teacher and several other women were trying to keep them occupied. Will told the children how good they had done and that he wanted them to behave for the ladies.

Gabe and Calvin hugged him before he left again.

"You boys help as much as you can, okay? I'm counting on you both."

The boys beamed with pride as they nodded.

He made his way to the hotel next, knowing this was where the gangs intended on meeting. He entered through the front door, hearing several guns click as they were cocked. "It's me, Will!"

Several men showed themselves from different areas of the lobby and dining room.

What he wasn't expecting to see was Sophie and the cook stepping out from a nook near the kitchen.

"Sophie! This wasn't the plan! Why are you here?"

She smiled and pointed to the area where she and the cook had been hunkered down. Will peeked around to see what she was pointing at. Shocked, he almost smiled.

"You have an entire arsenal! But you still can't stay. No. There's no way."

"Will, I need to greet my guests. They are my family, after all."

"No, Sophie. This is too dangerous."

About that time, one of the men near the front window called out that their guests had arrived.

Will quickly pushed her back in her nook and kissed her. "You be careful. Don't be taking any chances."

He had to try to think about his duty and not about the danger his wife had just put herself in.

Making his way back out through the kitchen door, he crept down the alley to watch as the gang arrived.

Junior was somewhat skeptical when everything appeared so quiet. He reasoned that it was probably too cold for most women to be out, it was a school day for children and a work day for most men.

The deputy was dressed casually and appeared to be running the hotel desk as Junior and three of his men stepped in.

"Morning, gentlemen. How can I help you?"

Junior walked to the desk. "We are looking for Sophie Collins."

"Oh, she was the previous owner. I bought this fine establishment from her recently, and she moved on."

"What?"

"Yes, sir. I'm sorry that you missed her. But since you are here, you may as well stay a while, perhaps have a meal. We aren't busy this time of year and only cook as needed, but we would be glad to fix you up. Perhaps some coffee?"

He was trying his best to get the men deeper into the lobby so they could surround them.

Junior nodded his head as he and the three men made their way to the dining room. He needed to make another plan, but he guessed he should stay put until he talked to Boss and Sonny.

Men stepped out from all angles and disarmed them quietly. The deputy went to the back door and nodded to Will.

"Drop your guns!" Will called as he rounded the corner. The three men went for their guns instead, and shots rang out about the time Sonny and his gang were entering town.

As Sonny's gang entered, wagons were pulled across both ends of the street, blocking a quick exit from town. For long moments, a major gunfight happened in the street.

Finally, everything went quiet. Will and several men started closing in on the men left standing and checking the ones that were fallen in the street.

"Throw down your guns," Will yelled. The men hesitantly complied. He led them to a jail cell saved just for them, quickly returning to the street for a head count.

All of the men from the town and his bounty hunters were accounted for except for Duff, who had left earlier to tend to the wagon train. Some of them were wounded but not seriously.

"How many men came in with each gang?"

"I counted ten in the second gang, Sheriff."

Another man called out, "There were seven with the first one."

"Okay, somebody get a count on the dead and wounded here while I get the ones from the hotel."

Buffalo meandered up. "I got one and one here."

Will looked past Buffalo to see one alive and one dead on horses tied to the post in front of the jail. When he looked back at Buffalo, he saw the big man unsheathe his huge knife and start cleaning blood off the blade with a look of satisfaction on his face. He just shook his head and made his way to the hotel.

Sophie was sitting in the dining room just a few feet from Junior, crying as he almost begged her to just shoot him instead of sending him to jail.

"It's the least you can do for me since all of this is your fault in the first place!"

Will hurried to her and held her. He looked at Junior and snapped gruffly, "Shut your mouth! Don't you talk to my wife."

"Wife?" he smirked. "Oh my! Apparently you are stupid or deceived."

Will took his huge fist and slugged him in the jaw, knocking him from his chair to the floor. "I said shut your mouth!"

He motioned for the deputy and the other men. "Get them out of here before I lose my temper."

Sophie cried against his shoulder for long moments. He kissed her tears away and held her close.

Finally, she assured him that she was okay. "I know you have a lot to do. Is it okay for me to tell the children to come out of the cellar?"

157

"Let me get a final count first and make sure we got them all." He kissed her tenderly. "I love you, Sophie."

Will got the final total of the gang members...one was missing. Sonny. He left the jail, wondering where he could be and if it was safe for everyone to come out of hiding. His decision was made when Duff came riding into town, slumped over his horse, dead.

Sonny must have made it out of town and to the wagon train. Will needed to go check and make sure everyone else was okay. He gathered several men to ride with him and told Sophie to start spreading the word that the danger had passed.

Chapter 14

Approaching the wagon train, Buffalo rode up beside Will. "This is about the smallest train I've ever seen. Something seems off."

Will nodded. "Yeah, I agree, especially so late in the season. Maybe they had trouble and the wagon master wouldn't wait on them."

"Maybe," Buffalo grunted and fell back a few steps.

A man rode out and met them. "We don't want any more trouble! Some crazy man already came through here, filled his saddlebags with food, and took off. He took a rifle from one of the women and slapped her."

"We aren't here for trouble, mister," Will assured. "I'm Sheriff Will Gentry, and we've come to give you an escort to town. I see you are a mite small to be out on your own. Can you tell me why?"

"We were with a bigger group, but it was getting on late in the season. We had run into trouble along the way. We decided to head this way to a town closer by to winter down, instead of staying with the group that was going to press on through the weather."

"I see. Probably a smart move. How many you got with you?"

"Two widows with six kids between them, my wife, two kids, and me."

"Just one man?"

"Yes, I couldn't let them strike out on their own, especially since I agreed it was the smart thing to do."

Will motioned for some of his men to take a look in the wagons and the surrounding area. "Sir, we are looking for a wanted criminal, so I hate to look through your wagons, but it is necessary."

The man motioned him to do what he wanted.

Pulling into town a while later, the women and children seemed grateful to have a nice warm room and food, hurrying in while some of the men took care of their horses.

Sophie was filled with compassion for them. She sat and chatted with the women as they ate, watching as her boys struck up a friendship with the other children.

One of the widows asked to be excused to get her journal out of her wagon, parked right in the alley. While she was gone, Sophie continued to chat with the other women. The other widow told Sophie how they couldn't wait to get to Colorado, where they had family waiting for them.

When the other widow returned minutes later, she sat and resumed the conversation while the other two women excused themselves to start getting the children ready for bed.

"I wanted to show you this before we retire for the evening. This is where we are going." She pulled out a newspaper clipping, handing it to Sophie.

Sophie read it and immediately knew something was wrong. Perhaps the women just didn't agree on their destination yet and Sophie wasn't going to stick her nose in their business. The newspaper clipping clearly stated Oregon.

She mentioned the discrepancy to Will as they settled into bed that night. He tried to discourage her from thinking bad thoughts, even though that's exactly what he was thinking.

When her breathing was soft and even, letting him know she was asleep, he slipped out of bed, dressed quickly, and went to find his men.

They stood outside of the jail and talked for a few minutes with Will explaining all he knew so far.

"You worry too much!" one of the men laughed. "You think we ain't done this before? Hmph. I couldn't tell you the last time any of us slept with both eyes shut.

"Go on back to bed. Manny is up in a tree somewhere, Buffalo is, well, who knows, but he ain't sleeping for sure. We don't ever let our guard down, especially right after something like this, when somebody is missing and one of our own dead."

Will went back to the hotel and quietly locked the front door, heading for the stairs. He heard a scuffle and started up the stairs two at a time. When he turned at the landing halfway up, he saw Sophie and another woman fighting at the top of the stairs.

Just as he started up, he saw that the woman was holding Sophie from behind with her arm around her neck. Suddenly, Sophie flipped the woman over her shoulder and down the stairs.

Will reached down and pulled the woman to her feet, holding her arms behind her. "What's going on here?" he demanded.

Sophie was bent over, trying to catch her breath. "She sneaked in our room and pulled a knife on me, Will. She's Sonny's wife!"

Will took her downstairs and found some rope to bind her hands and feet while he went to get the other woman, who he assumed was Junior's wife, and the couple that was with them, who was probably part of the gang also.

It was a long, sleepless night.

The next morning, Will sent a telegram to the U.S. Marshal again, telling him to come quickly before the snow set in, to pick up five dead, five wounded, eleven arrested, and eight children. The last words were: All Denny gang in custody except Sonny.

****

Will and Sophie were finally able to settle into a normal life with the boys. Sophie, who didn't care too much for all the snow, didn't even seem to mind it this year, she had Will and her boys, and that was all that mattered.

They were able to spend long days together, usually without interruption. This time of year, there was no one in the hotel and barely anyone in the diner.

Even Will's job, which started out in such a flurry of activity, had dwindled to practically nothing. The deputies knew they could find him at the hotel if he was needed.

School had let out for Christmas vacation with the teacher sending extra work home to last them through the months of January and February if the weather got bad enough to close the school.

Will decided to surprise the boys a few days before Christmas by making good on his word about something.

"I found something very interesting," he said over supper. He grinned mischievously at the boys.

"What, Pa?" they asked in unison.

"I found the perfect place to hunt for deer. You should have seen all of those deer tracks! I just wondered if I could find someone to go with me because I sure wouldn't want to go alone."

The boys' faces turned to nothing but wide eyes and smiles. They chattered on in excitement for a long time. Sophie squeezed Will's hand and smiled at him. He was just what her boys needed, what the town needed, and definitely what she needed.

****

Christmas was the most joyous that Sophie or Will could ever remember having. They had received letters from Will's family wishing them a Merry Christmas, with hopes of visiting them in spring.

As they enjoyed a nice venison roast on Christmas day, Gabe said he hoped school would resume soon so he could tell all the boys that his pa took him hunting. Calvin was more interested in the toys and candy he had found in his sock.

Will and Sophie sat back on the couch in front of the lobby fireplace and watched the boys play while basking in the love they had for each other.

"Sweetheart, what would you think about us having a real house of our own? I mean, the hotel is nice, but, I don't like sharing my home with so many people.

"We could live close by, or I could even add on to the back of the hotel, but just have a private place of our own."

Sophie gazed into his eyes. "I've always wanted that, but always felt it was too much to ask."

"Well then, I will get to work on some plans." He kissed her gently.

****

Gabe got his wish of going back to school long enough to tell about his hunting trip, then a few days

164

later, the bottom fell out of the sky. A blizzard hit them and snowed constantly for six days straight.

Will spent most of his days going to check on people to make sure they had everything they needed. He was thankful that most of his townsfolk believed in watching out for their neighbors, making his job much easier.

The end of January brought a round of sickness to the family and several other families, keeping the doctor busy with house calls. First, it was Calvin, then before he got well, it was Gabe, then Sophie got it.

By the middle of February, the boys were feeling better, and Sophie was just starting to get up and around. They sat in the lobby around the fireplace, helping the boys with schoolwork one morning right after breakfast.

Sophie felt sick again and rushed through the kitchen and out the back door. Will followed her. After a few minutes, she assured him she was feeling better and to just give her a moment. He kissed her cheek and returned to the boys.

Sophie put on a pot of tea before returning to the lobby. As she opened the door, she heard voices and walked silently and slowly to find out what was going on.

She peeked around the corner and saw an unbelievably horrible sight…Sonny was standing there holding one arm around Calvin's neck while holding a gun to her son's head.

Fear engulfed her, then rage. She slowly backed up and reached into the nook where she kept a couple of rifles, loaded and ready.

Sonny was demanding that he would trade Calvin for Sophie, and Will was trying to talk some sense into him.

Sophie could stand no more. She summoned her courage and steadied her hands, then stepped around the corner with the rifle aimed at Sonny.

"Let my boy go! NOW!"

Sonny hesitated too long to suit her. When he started to bring the gun from Calvin and in her direction, she pulled the trigger, hitting Sonny in the right side of his chest. He staggered a bit but still held to his gun and Calvin.

"Let him go!" She was out of patience, and seeing the fear in her son's eyes, pushed her over the edge. She pulled the trigger again, hitting him in his left shoulder.

Sonny's arm dropped, and Calvin ran to Will.

He feebly lifted the gun in her direction, and she hit him right through the center of his chest. With Sonny falling to the floor, Will walked over and kicked the gun out of his reach.

Sophie put the gun down as the boys ran to her. She wrapped her arms around them and kissed them over and over. Her heart was beating so hard, and her breath so shallow that she felt faint. She plopped down on the floor, still holding her boys, when darkness overtook her.

****

Sophie awoke on the couch with Will at her side, rubbing her face and holding her hand.

"The boys ran to get the doctor."

She started to get up, and he stopped her.

"Where's Sonny?"

"Sweetheart, you gave him plenty of warning, but he wouldn't listen. I'm sorry."

Her eyes glistened with tears as she laid back, unable to form words.

The doctor came in with the boys and Will helped her to their room where the doctor could examine her.

A little while later, the doctor came out, finding Will and the two boys standing in the hallway together.

"She's going to be fine, Will. What she just went through was highly unusual, especially just getting over the sickness. Just let her rest up a few days and she should be as good as new."

****

A few days later, Sophie was back to normal, fixing a feast of a supper, complete with dessert; a cake with white icing.

She covered the cake before anyone saw it, then called them all for supper. The conversation over supper consisted of plans for the new addition for their house come spring, the anticipation of Will's family coming to visit, Will taking the boys fishing when it got warm, and what kind of yarn Sophie needed for some projects.

Will looked at her oddly. "I didn't know you took time to do that kind of thing. Well, it is still winter, so I guess we will get you some yarn if that's what you want.

"What are you going to make? A new warm scarf for me?"

"Umm, no. Something smaller."

Gabe piped up, "One for me?"

"Umm, no. Something smaller."

"It's for me!" Calvin enthused.

Sophie stood and said, "No, something smaller." She uncovered the cake that had a silver baby spoon stuck in the center and raised her eyebrows at Will.

For a moment he was dumbfounded, then it hit him. He jumped up and shouted as he took her in his arms and swung her around.

"Oh, sweetheart! This is the best news ever!" He kissed her excitedly before turning to the boys and explaining what was going to happen.

The boys joined in the excitement of having a new little brother or sister.

"Will, you need to invite your ma to stay for the summer. As badly as she has wanted grandchildren, between the boys and this baby coming in July, there's no way she is going home for a long while."

"Looks like I need to rethink those house plans."

"What? An extra room for the baby?"

"Well, that too, but I meant a room for my folks. There's no way they are ever going to leave!"

He kissed her again. "I guess I've found my purpose, Sophie. You, the boys, and this baby, have given me purpose and I couldn't be any happier. I love you so much."

"And I love you, Will, with all my heart. I fought it for a while, but I could never deny it. You were so right about a marriage needing to have romance, and I will never regret the day you began to teach me all about it."

Enjoy all the adventures in this series!
https://www.amazon.com/Sheriff-Sophie-Lynne-Lanning-ebook/dp/B0C5GFWJZK

If you have enjoyed this book, please leave a review on Amazon.com, Goodreads, or any of your favorite book hangouts!

https://www.amazon.com/Sheriff-Sophie-Lynne-Lanning-ebook/dp/B0C5GFWJZK

Be the first to know about
new releases, cover reveals,
exclusive contests and much more,
when you sign up for my newsletter
LynneLanning.com

Books by Lynne Lanning

Desires of the Heart Series:
https://www.amazon.com/gp/product/B08P29PND5

1. Where He Leads:
2. I Surrender All
3. Trust And Obey
4. Just As I Am
5. Have Thine Own Way
6. It Is Well
7. Amazing Grace

Darnell Farms Series:
https://www.amazon.com/gp/product/B0B8X38JDD

1. Promises of Love
2. Whirlwinds of Turmoil
3. Seasons of Change
4. Dawn of Humility
5. Horizons of Reconciliation
6. Untitled – coming late 2023

Stand-Alone Books Within Multiple Author Projects:
The Matchmaker – Agatha Returns Entire Series:
https://www.amazon.com/gp/product/B0BB6KDT5H

Lynne Lanning's Book in the Series:
A Match for Korban:
https://www.amazon.com/gp/product/B0BN36KN2P

Rescue Me (Mail-Order Brides) Entire Series:
https://www.amazon.com/gp/product/B0BKLNTH1N
Lynne Lanning's Books in the Series:
Josie:
https://www.amazon.com/gp/product/B0BJZ5Z979
Layla:
https://www.amazon.com/gp/product/B0BJZLPP5Z

Hers To Redeem – The Reclusive Man Entire Series:
https://www.amazon.com/gp/product/B0BNKN43TP
Lynne Lanning's Book in the Series:
Jody's Journey: https://www.amazon.com/Jodys-Journey-Hers-Redeem-Reclusive-ebook/dp/B0BRTK9LY4

Stay in touch! Several more books scheduled for 2023 and 2024! Sign up for Lynne's newsletter at LynneLanning.com Christian Romance Author | Lynne Lanning

Dear Friend,

I hope this book has been an inspiration and a joy to read. If you are perhaps looking for a church, or for spiritual help, please feel free to contact our church. Other than traditional church services, we also have online services and radio broadcasts.

Trinity Baptist Church

2722 U.S. Hwy. 601 South
Mocksville, NC   27028
336-284-2404

Trinitybaptistchurchnc.org

Preacher Darrell Cox

49039704R10096